I0655635

The Harlequin
of Pizza County

THE HARLEQUIN
OF PIZZA COUNTY

A NOVEL BY

STEPHEN
TANNENBAUM

Red Engine Press
Fort Smith, Arkansas

COPYRIGHT © 2023 BY STEPHEN TANNENBAUM

ALL RIGHTS RESERVED. NO PART OF THIS BOOK MAY BE REPRODUCED OR TRANS-MITTED IN ANY FORM OR BY ANY MEANS, ELECTRONIC OR MECHANICAL, INCLUDING PHOTOCOPYING, RECORDING, OR BY ANY INFORMATION STORAGE AND RETRIEVAL SYSTEM (EXCEPT BY A REVIEWER OR COMMENTATOR WHO MAY QUOTE BRIEF PASSAGES IN A PRINTED OR ON-LINE REVIEW) WITHOUT PERMISSION FROM THE PUBLISHER.

COVER ART COPYRIGHT © 2023 ANA (KAT) GALLY ZELAYA

LIBRARY OF CONGRESS CONTROL NUMBER: 2023949371

ISBN: 979-8-9879576-8-4

Dedication

The author wishes to dedicate this book, as he has dedicated the others, to his mentor, Monty Culver, with whom he had the good fortune to have studied fiction writing for almost twenty years.

The author wishes he could find sufficient words to thank his wife Shirley for applying her talents as editor to the text of "The Harlequin," and for her infinite patience in dealing with the author, which she has done for more than sixty-four years.

Also by Stephen Tannenbaum

Novels

Cloris Hughes
Complications
The Invisible Man of Pizza County

THE HARLEQUIN
OF PIZZA COUNTY

A NOVEL

Chapter 1

He is desperate or he wouldn't be here.

The person who will soon be renown as the Harlequin throughout western Pennsylvania's Piazza County is hunkered down behind the wheel of his rust bucket of a vehicle; his eyes are on the glass front door of the *PNC Bank* branch. Parked across Ruffner Road in the shadows of the building that houses the *Dollar General*, he is no more than thirty or forty yards from that door.

The gender-defining pronoun, he, used by eyewitnesses is a presumption on their part; given the body coverage achieved by the disguises the Harlequin uses, it is difficult for them to tell for sure.

It is a struggle to climb into the flimsy clown costume while seated behind the wheel, trying to avoid snagging a shoe on the costume's flimsy plastic pants legs; it is like a wrestling match with his own arms and legs. With his body finally in the costume, the Harlequin dabs perspiration from his forehead and reaches for his stage makeup kit. He applies stark white to all visible surfaces of his face, over the white goes red to the cheeks, blue circles around each eye, and a red putty ball on the tip of his nose. Pulled over his head and ears is a stringy, orange fright wig.

Not an ideal time to apply face makeup when your hands are shaking with the adrenaline of anticipation and, to be honest, fear. The Harlequin examines himself in the rear-view mirror—the costume is raggedy, he admits, but he is satisfied it will achieve the desired effect: no one will be frightened, more likely they will be amused by his appearance, so no one will scream or do anything else stupid. And even his mother looking down from Heaven isn't likely to recognize him.

Ruffner Road enters Pizza County from the south, and near the center of the County it skirts Sutersberg's east side and heads north. One can get anywhere reasonably well in the County using Ruffner Road, as long as you aren't in a hurry. It is a two-lane strip of cracked asphalt that takes its good old time wandering among the farms and rural communities on its winding way north.

Right up the road from the strip that includes the bank, a hardware store and the Dollar General, there is a lonesome-looking model McMansion and an area staked out in lots for a neighborhood of McMansions that never materialized. There seems to be no future for McMansions on Ruffner Road, and not much future for any of the businesses on it, either. But at this moment it seems to the Harlequin to be the perfect site for a bank robbery.

He surveilles the area once again and suddenly it isn't perfect. A woman wrapped in a hooded anorak climbs out of her car and removes a bundle from the back seat, a child swaddled tightly in a blanket. She juggles a purse, the blanketed bundle of child and a remote to lock the car, nearly dropping the bundle. She heaves the child over her shoulder and pushes through the glass door into the bank. Rats! Oh, well. He thought to bring with him a single lollipop he intended to present to the bank teller along with a note demanding money. He will have to give it—the lollipop, not the note—to the child. He hopes the child won't start screaming, but he isn't confident. The Harlequin remembers being chased by killer clowns from outer space in nightmares when he was a child.

Employing an exaggerated leaping, prancing gait, he heads toward the bank. Halfway across Ruffner Road a gust of wind sweeps him up and nearly carries him off his feet, the flimsy costume billowing like a sail. He stops in the middle of the traffic-less road to chastise the wind and yell angrily at the sky. Like all western Pennsylvanians, the Harlequin is in the habit of complaining about the weather all the time, usually for good reason: it is either too hot or too cold, too damp or too dry, too windy or too still. He loves to grouse at the sky and the weatherman and...whoever.

Still standing in the middle of the road, the Harlequin admits, "To be fair, the weather is rarely if ever life threatening, unlike other places you hear about or read about, but still..."

He more than other people has a legitimate complaint: For instance, yesterday he woke up to a thirty-six-degree morning with a predicted high of fifty-eight degrees. In January. This morning, on the other hand, it is a windy twenty degrees, and he is freezing his ass off in a lousy clown costume that refuses to fit over a heavy coat. Standing in the middle of Ruffner Road, he puts it to the sky this way:

"How was I to know what to wear to work today, huh? How was I to know?"

Chapter 2

Initial meeting- Harlequin Task Force
Sutersberg, PA
July 17

The air temperature in Piazza County on this Friday afternoon in July had climbed into the high eighties. It threatened to climb higher and backed up the threat with stifling humidity. But in the conference room on the third floor of the County Courthouse Annex, the temperature was arctic.

The conference room: a fifteen by twenty rectangle, carpeted, a floor-to-ceiling wall of windows facing out to Sutersberg's South Main Street; a nine-foot conference table of polished walnut in the shape of an Asian eye, and eight matching chairs with leather cushions; also matching the table, a walnut credenza draped with a narrow cloth holding several dozen bottles of drinking water; in the far corner of the room, a stack of wooden folding chairs in case of an overflow of attendees. All told, a room more than adequate for the initial meeting of this special task force, except for the absence of a thermostat. The temperature was arctic.

The conferees' first thoughts on reaching the third-floor conference room being for their own personal comfort, they—mostly male suits, a few uniforms, two women— climbed out of their suit coats and uniform blouses and draped them over the backs of their chairs before mingling or seating themselves. Almost immediately they found it necessary to struggle out of their chairs and climb back into their coats. The older of the two women, obviously familiar with the foibles of the Annex building, ignored the outside temperature and came prepared with a bulky knitted cardigan that she draped over her shoulders.

Federal agent Ed Plunkett, having eschewed the conference table for a folding chair in a far back corner of the room, was in an unsettled mood. Wooden folding chairs are hard on the ass, true enough, but Ed Plunkett had more urgent concerns: he was more than normally affected by the temperature in the room because it reminded him of the cold, hard operating table and arctic temperature in the surgical suite of Pittsburgh's Presbyterian Hospital. Surgeons there had recently dug a nine-mm slug out of his abdomen. How miserable he remembered feeling in that surgical suite, like a naked slab of meat in a frozen food locker. Plunkett's wife, Edna, might have become a widow—Ed's abdominal wound was that serious. Except Edna had already deserted him, the divorce was final a year prior to the shooting.

After surviving the surgery, followed by convalescent leave and rehab, Agent Plunkett was allowed to return to duty—light duty only for... maybe indefinitely. Plunkett, a six-footer and former high school track star, now with an imagination as wounded as his body, thought of himself as The Incredible Shrinking Man, with a hunch in his upper back, a stomach that sometimes heaved unpredictably and an expanded waistline. In addition, he imagined his future with the FBI spiraling down into a dumpster. He knew of other agents whose careers had plopped into that same dumpster due to health issues. Some had become desk jockeys, others were out.

It would help everyone's career, especially his own, he thought, if this task force were able to achieve its intended goal. But what were the odds on that? This bunch of nobodies and clowns capture the Pizza County

5

Harlequin? He couldn't help sniggering as he watched his fellow task force members struggle with the temperature in the frigid room. Could they succeed at any task? They represented a lot of years in law enforcement, true enough, but were they good years or were they simply time served?

Plunkett realized brains were the commodity needed to catch the Harlequin, and he saw no evidence of good working brains in that room; not at the moment, anyway.

Two cowboy look-alikes pushed into the room: a tall, thin one wearing a ten-gallon hat, western-style boots and a holstered firearm tied to his thigh with rawhide. Wyatt f-ing Earp. Earp was in the company of a fat one, a real five by five, who entered the room with flash and noise, as if he were a visiting dignitary. Both men were wearing the black trousers and short-sleeved, white summer uniform blouses of the Sutersberg Police Department. Fatty sported a silver star on his shirt to identify himself as the chief.

As soon as Deputy Earp saw his chief comfortably seated at the conference table, he sauntered with hat in hand toward the corner of the room where Agent Plunkett was seated. Plunkett admired the abundance of the deputy's thick black hair. It was piled onto the very top of his head and the sides were clipped in the latest fashion, down to scalp. Sure, he looked as if he had been clipped with a pudding bowl over his head. Laughable, still...Plunkett was immediately aware of and was alarmed by the deputy's sinister aura. His neck was wide as his head, and there was a prominent, bony ridge of forehead that sheltered a pair of deeply-set snake's eyes. With reservations as to whether he would ever get his hand back, Plunkett offered it to the deputy in greeting.

He said, "Ed Plunkett, FBI. Welcome to the, uh, the Harlequin task force."

The deputy hesitated, as if what he was about to say was a secret. Finally, "Perkins. Poke Perkins. Sergeant, Sutersberg cops. Gladameecha." Perkins asked, "That yer boss up there?"

"That's him, yeah. In the blue suit."

Perkins suspected Plunkett of putting him on. He glanced at the men standing toward the front then returned his eyes to Plunkett and said, "They're all in blue suits." The FBI agent felt caught in a cobra's glare and he, Plunkett, was its prey.

Plunkett swallowed and said, "Red tie. That's Assistant AIC Sparks." He explained that AIC was an acronym for Agent in Charge.

Perkins sneered; he knew that. Then he said, "Something's wrong with his throat."

Assistant AIC Sparks stood at the head of the conference table repeatedly clearing his throat. His attempts at calling the meeting to order were being ignored. Intentionally, he was sure.

Sparks called out, "We're all present now, gentlemen, ladies. Let's get underway."

No discernible response.

"Aw, c'mon, guys. Nobody wants to be here on a Friday afternoon, I know that. I don't either. But there's a couple beers with our names on them just waiting for us down at Mr. Frog's. So, let's get started. The sooner we do, the sooner we get to those beers."

Murmurs of agreement and curses were mixed with remarks about beers, about Mr. Frog's, about Friday afternoons. The attendees all grabbed seats at or near the table and came to order.

"Well now, that's better," Sparks said. "Let's get started."

Chapter 3

A gent Sparks surveyed the crowd.

He said, "We all know each other, right? Are introductions necessary? No…yes? Well, okay, I'll start with myself. I'm Perry John Sparks, FBI, Assistant Agent in Charge of the Pittsburgh field office. Friends call me Jack. You can, if you like. I've been appointed head of the task force. My colleague from the Bureau is sitting in back there, somewhere. Where are you, Ed? Raise yer hand. There, Ed Plunkett, folks. Ed and I are both western Pennsylvania boys, but not from around here, from the other side of the 'burgh.

"Now, this lovely lady…" Sparks said, indicating the older of the two women in the room, the one with the bulky cardigan over her shoulders and gray hair in a bun. He pretended to know her, but he was palming a three-by-five card with notes. "…name of Hannigan, Livia Hannigan. She's a longtime staff member of the Pizza County D.A.'s Office. She'll record all our meetings and keep the white board up to date."

People looked around, there was no white board.

"There's no white board!" Perkins called from the back.

"There will be," Sparks replied, "when we have something to put on it. Now, if it's okay, I'll continue with the intros."

"It's okay," Perkins called.

"Shut up, Poke, fer godsake," his chief, Mr. Five by Five, ordered.

Sparks resumed, "We got reps from the DA's offices of three different counties. First, our other distaff member, Marge Bash, Assistant DA from here in Pizza County."

Ed Plunkett thought, I'm told, it used to be only the locals called it Pizza County rather than its actual name, Piazza County, but now everybody does.

Sparks said, "Stand up, Marge."

Marge Bash stood. She was a thirty-something and a looker. She looked purposely dressed down, wearing a dark gray business suit with a knee-length pencil skirt and a narrow-lapelled, matching jacket over a white blouse. Streaked blond hair and large, plastic-framed glasses tried to put finishing touches on the cover up. Bash spread a weak smile that lacked enthusiasm around the room before retaking her seat.

Sparks said, "Next we got ADA Bert Dixon...no?" He stole a peek at his notes. "It's Dix-ton, isn't it. Bert Dixton from Fayette County."

Dixton, also a thirty-something, stood. A former football player or a wrestler, by the look of him. Accent on the word former, but Dixton still looked capable of bench pressing two or three hundred pounds. At the moment he looked as if he wanted to bench press Marge Bash. Dixton tossed off a wave and sat back down.

"The third DA is our old buddy from Allegheny County, Tony Cechetti."

Cechetti waved from his chair. He was another former footballer, but a lot more former than Dixton.

Plunkett thought, Cechetti looks worn out and long in the tooth. Longer in the tooth than me.

Sparks then moved his attention to the uniforms, most of whom were seated around the table. He said, "In the dress blue uniform of the Pittsburgh Police, Assistant Chief Lawrence Langford. Larry will act as liaison between us and the other police departments, keeping them all informed and, we hope, involved. Right, Larry?"

Larry stood with the intention of expressing at length his hopes along that line, but Agent Sparks shushed him, so Larry sat down.

Sparks flashed an open hand toward Mr. Five by Five, who was overwhelming the chair next to Larry. He said, "Is there anybody in the room doesn't know Dom Ianuzzi, Chief of the Sutersberg Police? I don't think so, but what the hell. Stand up anyway, Nuzzi, give that chair a breather."

That got chuckles from the group, from Nuzzi, too, only it didn't spread very far across his broad face. His belly wobbled. Nuzzi, his voice a fraction or two higher pitched than expected from such a large man, welcomed the attendees to Pizza County, his County, then introduced his sergeant, who lurked in the far corner behind Agent Plunkett. At the call of his name, Perkins took a large step forward and touched two fingers to the brim of his Stetson in salute to the group, then lurked back into the corner.

Next, cops from The State Police force and from small towns all over the three involved counties were introduced. Finally, Sparks looked around the room and recognized that there was no one left to recognize. He breathed a sigh of relief.

He said, "Now that we all know who we are, let's get a start on doing our job, which is to find out who in Hell the Pizza County Harlequin is."

Chapter 4

Once he knew the room was finally his, Sparks began.

He said, "Our timeline begins last December. In the week before Christmas our perp hit two small, mostly drive-thru type bank branches, one in Lower Burrell, Pizza County, the other just east of Connellsville, Fayette County. Both times disguised as Santa Claus."

ADA Marge Bash grumbled, "That shouldn't count for them, it should count for us. Connellsville's on the eastern edge of Fayette County, I mean on the very edge. Hell, a drunk losing his balance in Connellsville could fall on his ass and find he's landed in Pizza County. We should get credit for two robberies."

Sparks sighed as Bash blithered, realizing why DA Grimes of Pizza County had dumped Bash on the task force.

Bash blithered on, "Besides, the take of both robberies combined was less than two hundred bucks and change. I'd gladly reimburse the banks their two hundred if my boss would release me from this damn task force and let me go on my vacation. I got reservations at Niagara Falls."

Sparks made a mental note to ignore the woman from then on. He said, "Your point is well taken, Ms Bash, Santa didn't get much in Connellsville or Lower Burrell. And not much in his next caper, either, but it's that next caper, the third, that the shit first hit the fan, if you'll excuse my French. For that next caper he dresses like a clown and he hits the *PNC* branch in Hempfield Township." He looked at ADA Bash and said, "Credit again goes to Pizza County."

One of the small-town cops from Allegheny County asked if Sparks was referring to the *PNC* branch near Greenfield Mall. Sparks asked Ms Hannigan to check her notes. She corrected the cop, telling him, first, that Greenfield Mall no longer existed, it had been torn down and replaced years ago, and second, the branch he was referring to hadn't been hit until right before Easter. The bank branch Agent Sparks was referring to, the one hit in January, was the *PNC* branch located next to the *Dollar General* on Ruffner Road.

"Right," said Sparks. "Thanks for that, Ms Hannigan. Now when… what?" One of the men assigned to the task force from the Pennsylvania State Police, Trooper Jon Stepinski, had a question.

Stepinski had been working out of the Sutersberg Barracks of the State cops for five years, so he was a known quantity to Pizza Countians. They had, as was their habit, slapped a nickname, Stump, on Stepinski mostly in fun and friendship, never meaning harm. They called him Stump, although he was a very tall, strapping, imposing figure. Stepinski had no clue as to why they called him Stump, but he didn't mind it. He was no rookie, he was into his seventh year on the Pennsylvania State Police force. He was a conscientious, dutiful cop who unfortunately was a little mentally shy of a load.

Stepinski stood, which took a while to unwind his lanky frame. He said, "I was just wondering, Is there an Upper Burrell? There's a Lower Burrell, we all know that, so it stands to reason there must be an Upper Burrell, too. Well, don't it?"

"Don't it what?"

"Don't it stand to reason, there must be an Upper Burrell?"

"What the fuck difference does it..." Sparks stopped himself. "Excuse my French again, Ms Hannigan. Marge. I'm tryin' to make this quick, everybody moaning it's Friday afternoon, and you wanna know is there an Upper Burrell. Well, I don't know if there's an Upper Burrell and I don't give a shit. Now, can I get on with this? Thanks.

"When I said the shit hit the fan with the third robbery, it did, it hit it and hard, but not because of a big haul. As Ms Bash was so kind to point out, the take was small there, too, just as small as Lower Burrell and Connellsville. No, the shit hit the fan because some son of a bitch dubbed the perp the Harlequin, making him seem like Zorro or Robin Hood or some other hero like that, and making the local cops out as horse's asses for not being able to nab him. The Harlequin's total take in a dozen robberies wouldn't pay any of our salaries for a month..."

Speak for yourself, boss, Plunkett thought, knowing some of the local boys weren't paid very much.

"...Believe me, the amount of each take isn't what our task force is all about," Sparks continued, "It's about pride, it's about our individual and collective reputations, and how we're thought of by the public and the media. The guy that named our perp the Harlequin did us no favor. Fact, I'd like to get my hands on him, whoever he is. Chief?" Nuzzi's fat hand was up.

He said, "I can help with that, I know the guy. Everybody in Pizza County knows the guy, at least everybody what hangs around the Courthouse knows him. Everybody what shops the supermarkets and the stores around Sutersberg knows him, too. Name of Harry Samuels. They call him Harry S."

Under his breath Sergeant Perkins whispered, "Hairy ass," which meant everyone in the room heard it.

Nuzzi called back to his minion, "Shut yer pie hole, Poke." Then back to Agent Sparks, "Harry Samuels puts out a weekly shopper thing, y'know? Ads and coupons, mostly supermarkets and drug stores, that kinda crap. Harry thinks he's a hot shot newsman. Excuse me, a journalist. Hah! The *Weekly Wise Shopper*, he calls it. But it's true enough, Harry S gets credit for the name, the Pizza County Harlequin. Harry claims he was on the scene cashing a check in the *PNC* on Ruffner Road when the guy dressed like a clown hit the place. Put his eyewitness account on the front page of the *Weekly Wise Shopper*. Called him the Harlequin right up front and there's been an article about the Harlequin in every edition since that first one, about how the Harlequin is so clever and how we can't catch him. Can you believe it? Ole Harry S."

"Making you look like a Horse's ass, Nuzzi," said Cechetti, the ADA from Allegheny County. "Making us all look like a horse's ass."

Nods and grunts of agreement from the assembled crowd.

"And," added Agent Sparks, "making the Governor get on my boss's ass, who then got on my ass to head up this task force. The politicians are in this big time, so you can believe it's our collective ass if we don't carry the ball into the end zone, if you don't mind a football reference. Well, alright, now you know our collective ass is on the line. What are we gonna do about it?" Sparks put on a game face and glowered at several members of the team. He asked, "Hmm? What are we?"

No one had a reply to offer.

❋ ❋ ❋

The members of the Harlequin task force were being filled in on the details of the other eight bank robberies perpetrated by their man, the Harlequin. The majority of witnesses were in agreement on only one thing, that the Harlequin was a man, but one or two of them weren't willing to swear to it on a stack of Bibles. At the very same time, the employees of the *VitaBank* branch in the Millton Shopping Center, each having returned from their lunch breaks, now were struggling to stay awake. Certainly things would pick up as soon as the day shifts at *Tool'nDie Foundry* and the *RockLite Brewery* let out. Until then it was yawnsville in the bank and in the entire shopping center.

Imagine their surprise when former President Richard Nixon, waving his arms and flashing a 'V' for victory with his fingers, and dressed for success in a blue suit and a snazzy red tie, barged through the door and announced his intention to make an immediate withdrawal.

✳ ✳ ✳

A commotion in the corridor outside of the conference room interrupted Agent Sparks in the middle of detailing for the task force members the last caper of the Harlequin, that being the robbery two weeks ago of the *Commonwealth Trust* branch in Leechburg. Sparks stopped talking altogether when the door cracked open wide enough for a young woman to poke her head through. It was the room she was looking for, obviously, because she came entirely in. She was a redhead; a twenty something who looked to be about five-foot-five or six tall and weighed about one hundred forty pounds—looking sharp in the white uniform blouse and dark blue trousers of the Sutersburg Police, but without ID patches on the sleeves or breast pockets.

Of course Chief Ianuzzi and Sergeant Perkins knew her; they both shouted at her, "Tessa, what are you..."

Nuzzi identified her to the room as Tessa Waugaman, his day shift dispatcher, a civilian employee.

She said, at the same time struggling for breath, "Yuns all got yer comms off," looking at her boss, "yer cell phones are off, too. I hadda run all the way up here to getcha. It's damn hot out there." She was flushed, breathless and damp with sweat. "Don't worry," she went on, panting, "Dunphy's coverin' for me."

Tessa noticed all the faces in the room were focused on her, all of them wondering where the fire was. "Millton's where," she said. "A Millton patrolman called it in, a robbery in the Laurel Mountain Center, y'know, off Route 30? The *VitaBank*. According to the cop, the perp was Richard Nixon. Smart ass guy, that cop. I told him I thought he was pullin' my leg..." She had her breath more in control now and she seemed less intimidated by the number of suits and uniforms in the room. "... and he says to me, he'd love to pull my leg but no foolin', the bank employees swear the perp was Richard Nixon."

"The Harlequin," somebody shouted followed by several shouts of agreement followed by people leaping to their feet, followed by a stampede of uniforms for the door. Nuzzi among them. Sergeant Perkins managed to get in front of Nuzzi, clearing the way for the extra wide load.

Cooler heads prevailed among the suits. Except to call in a crime scene forensic team, there was little at the moment for DAs and federal agents to do. They remained in the room—not seated, mind, too much tension had been generated in the room to stay seated. They milled about, wagging their heads and making lip-smacking sounds. Even Ed Plunkett's folding chair felt electrically charged. He sauntered to the front of the room with his hands in his pockets and said to his boss, "Would you say the shit has hit the fan?"

Sparks replied, "Yes, I would. I'd say it has. It definitely has."

Chapter 5

The next morning early, a Saturday, Plunkett looked out of the window of his assigned room at the *Executive Motor Inn*. He faced a bright, fresh June morning that made him glad all over again that he had survived. He was still alive. He wondered if every agent after being shot had that thought in mind whenever he or she did something he had just done, simply looked out the window at a beautiful morning. He wondered too if he would ever be able to put it behind him.

He dressed, availed himself of what the management had the nerve to call a continental breakfast—tepid, coffee-colored water and stale Danish. What continent were they thinking of?

Plunkett drove his leased vehicle out of the motel parking lot, and in five minutes parked it in the multi-level garage attached to the Courthouse Annex in downtown Sutersberg. The distance between the motel and the Annex was little more than half a mile, walking distance and he could have used the exercise, but although at the moment the air was more breathable than it had been the day before—Plunkett thanked God for that—there was still a heaviness to the air that warned of another stifling afternoon. Soon he found himself standing in front of the Courthouse Annex. Main Street was ghostly quiet this early on a Saturday morning.

Ed Plunkett, early riser. He hadn't always been an early riser. It used to be his great pleasure to languish in bed, hitting the snooze alarm often, unable to tear himself out of the embracing arms of a warm bed. Until his encounter with death—a single slug in the stomach. That more than anything else he'd encountered in fifteen years in law enforcement made Plunkett an early riser. Once his eyes opened, no matter how early the clock said it was, he kept them open. To shut them again risked them staying shut forever.

To locate the business office of *The Weekly Wise Shopper* from the Courthouse and its Annex required only a little of Ed Plunkett's diligence and a little of his shoe leather. He located it on South Pennsylvania Avenue across from the Public Library, in a row of rather neglected-looking store fronts between the Army Recruiting Office and the Christian Science Reading Room.

Unknown to the federal agent, the site was previously the location of a failed pet grooming salon, but Plunkett's sense of smell was keen. Immediately on pushing through the door of the *Weekly Wise Shopper*, lingering hints of soap suds and dog hair tickled his nose.

Plunkett found himself in a bare-bones, claustrophobic, eight- by-ten-foot rectangular space. Two battered desks—from a used furniture store, the agent suspected—were placed side by side to occupy almost all of the floor space, leaving no room for anything or anyone else, including Plunkett. The lack of a bell to announce his arrival led him to conclude that no visitors were expected and none were wanted.

The only attempt at decorating the room had been done to the short wall on Plunkett's left: articles from the front pages of recent issues of the *Weekly Wise Shopper* were stuck to the bare plaster with adhesive tape.

A short passageway opposite the front door, too long to be called an alcove but too short for a hall, opened into a tiny washroom and a second space, too tiny to be called a room, that held what looked to Plunkett like some sort of artist's or draftsman's layout table and a computer. Crowded into the inadequate space and intent on something on the computer screen were a man and a woman; closeted as they were by the tiny space, their movements needed to be choreographed to prevent their bumping into each other. Or so it appeared to Plunkett from his position near the front door.

They hadn't heard or noticed his entry, so Plunkett rapped with a knuckle on one of the desks. Their response to the knock: the couple in the layout room looked up from their preoccupation, stared at each other in surprise, and then they turned to stare at him. With a nod of his head toward the front room—a male pattern bald head, like his own head would soon be, the agent thought. That's him, that must be Samuels.

The woman seemed unsure as to who was the designated greeter. The man Plunkett assumed was Harry Samuels indicated with a toss of the head that she was it. Reluctant as she was to accept the role, with a shrug, she did.

Plunkett's first impression as he was approached by this forty-something woman was that he was being approached hesitantly on tiptoes by a monk. She was wearing a muumuu of a dark brown, wooly material. There were no women monks, as far as he knew, so he wondered if she had once been a man. Probably not, but she proved to be almost as tall as the FBI man. Her dark hair, streaked with gray, looked as if it had been chopped rather than merely cut. Stitched on the muumuu she was wearing, instead of a pocket, was the name Helen sewn with blue thread.

She avoided looking directly at Plunkett, which seemed deliberate. He had yet to announce himself as a federal agent, but she already seemed ready to plead guilty. Her eyes were down or up, to the left or right. In an attempt to pin her eyes down, Plunkett found himself bobbing and weaving with her. He discovered that her eyes were a darker brown than the muumuu she was wearing, and they were pooled with moisture. And full of either sorrow or regret; Plunkett wasn't sure which, maybe both. What had he done to elicit such a reaction from her? He hadn't a clue. Something had caused him, a stranger, to happen into these premises, and whatever that something was, Helen was sorry for it.

Helen gazed over Plunkett's right shoulder and said, "Yes." Not a question but delivered as if she were answering a question put to her by someone lurking behind him. He spun around—no one was there. Damn, but this woman, Helen, gave him the willies. He took a couple breaths to calm himself, then produced his ID wallet and held it in front of her face. He said, "Ed Plunkett, FBI."

She replied, "Helen Waugaman," as if she were sorry about it, too.

"Waugaman, huh? That your sister I met yesterday, the civilian dispatcher?"

She replied, "Tessa," reluctantly, as if she weren't sure.

"Yeah, Tessa. Say, is that Harry Samuels back there?" Without waiting for a reply, Plunkett called toward the back room, "Hey, Mr. Samuels? It's Ed Plunkett, FBI. I'd like a word, if you don't mind?"

Samuels replied, sounding unhappy about it, that he would be right there.

Helen spoke the word "Saturday" as if she thought the FBI man couldn't possibly know what day it was because if he did know what day it was, he wouldn't have come today. She sounded as if his appearance at this particular time was a major disaster. What followed were a few disjointed phrases, such as the following: "Busy. Don't keep him. Layouts overdue at printers. Today, Saturday. Noon, the printer shop closes at noon." She stamped her foot.

The FBI man reassured her with a promise he wouldn't keep her boss more than a few minutes. A brief interview was all he required.

Harry Samuels came out of the back room and stood at the counter next to his employee; Helen seemed mountainous next to him. Not that Samuels was small, he was simply as average a man at five foot six or seven and maybe 160 pounds as Agent Plunkett had ever seen. But the two standing alongside each other seemed to meld together. That phenomenon made it difficult for Plunkett, even with his training and experience as an observer of people, to characterize Samuels.

Despite this difficulty, Plunkett observed a few things about Samuels that he thought seemed contradictory: for one thing, some local dentist with visions of Hollywood in mind had done a bleaching job on Samuels's teeth. Looking directly at him made the FBI man feel as if he had just been sold a used car.

To contradict that sleazy opinion of Samuels, what he was wearing gave the exact opposite impression: beige chinos, a sleeveless, collarless vest of a lightweight brown material that looked like polyester, and the clincher, a checkered buffalo shirt and a blue knitted necktie, no pattern. How long had it been since Plunkett had seen anyone wearing a buffalo shirt and a knitted tie? Was he just an individualist, this guy Samuels? Or was he dressed purposely to confuse everyone he met? Or was he merely a man with no fashion sense? Plunkett decided to postpone making a judgment and let time tell.

Samuels said, "Forgive me for not recognizing you right away, Agent Puckett. Without these glasses…" He drew a pair of rimless specs from his shirt pocket and put them on. "Getting old…"

"Plunkett."

"What?"

"Plunkett. The name is Plunkett, Ed Plunkett."

"Oh, sorry. Agent Plunkett. I recognize you now from last night's crime scene in Millton, and again at the press conference afterwards. I was there, too, in case you missed seeing me. I saw the two of you, you and your boss...Sparks, is it?"

"That was us, alright. The press conference wasn't our idea, blame that on, whatsisname, the chief of the Millton cops. There wasn't much of anything to see at the bank, and what could we say to the media: We don't know anything? You guys already knew we didn't know anything."

Samuels nodded his head in agreement. He turned to his employee, Helen Waugaman, and asked her to return to the computer and run a final spell check of the layouts before uploading them to the printer. He said, "While you're doing that, Agent Plunkett and I will step outside for a breath of air."

She seemed reluctant to leave her boss alone in the clutches of the FBI man. Perhaps the idea of working alone upset her, too.

Samuels placed a reassuring hand on her arm and said, "Now, don't get yourself in a nervy knot. You know you can do it. You've done it dozens of times, no need for me to be gawking over your shoulder. Off you go, now. Go, go." He shooed her toward the layout room at back. She didn't want to, but she went.

Samuels ushered his visitor out the door into a wall of heat that was waiting for them on the sidewalk. No traffic on Pennsylvania Avenue this early on a Saturday. They crossed toward the Public Library and headed for a bench in the shade of a maple tree that awaited their arrival.

Samuels remarked that it was his favorite spot, though a metal bench could be a bit hard on the ass. Plunkett replied, "No, no, this is nice. There's a breeze."

"There's always a breeze here."

"So, uh, can she...y'know, can she actually work that computer without screwing it up?"

"Who, Helen? With her you're never sure. She's got a lot of...shall we say, issues?"

"But you employ her because..."

"Because her salary is paid in full by a State program. Cheap is everything in my tenuous financial position." After a moment's pause, "But...if she does screw up, Agent Puckett, everything is backed up in the Cloud. To paraphrase Ronald Reagen: 'Trust, but cover your ass.' He actually said that. Or somebody did." Samuels tossed a hand in the air. "Besides, would it be earthshaking if something prevented the *Weekly Wise Shopper* from going to press?" He tossed that off again. "No one would miss it, except lately maybe they might miss reading my editorial on the front page."

Samuels had called him Puckett again. A common enough error, Plunkett mused, but also a sharp barb. Which had it been? He wasn't sure. He found it refreshing to watch the leaves on the maple tree as they stirred with the ebb and flow of the breeze.

He said, looking down directly at Samuels's jowly hound of a face, "If you don't mind my asking…" But hoping Samuels did mind, "It must be hard to swallow, y'know? A real comedown in the tail end of a long, successful career to find yourself operating back in the minor leagues. A shopper's weekly throw-away. No offense meant."

Samuels recognized the challenge and accepted it. He replied, "Is that a question for me or for you, yourself?" But his face was a mask of vulnerability. His cheeks showed an uncharacteristic flush and the crow's feet at the corners of his eyes became more prominent. It was only momentary but exchanging barbs with Plunkett appeared to age him several years. Guessing that Samuels was more vulnerable than he originally thought, Plunkett regretted using that classic interrogation technique on him.

Samuels shrugged off some of the tension; his voice took on a gruff note. He said, "A comedown, you say? Yeah, as if at the tail end of a long, successful career in law enforcement you found yourself employed as a school crossing guard. Yeah, I'd say comedown was the correct word."

Plunkett figured he owed Samuels an apology. He would have apologized if Samuels had given him time to do so, but he didn't. He went on, this time without any hint of retaliation in his voice: "My career, that long, successful career in Journalism you referred to before, started in Cleveland. Didn't you look me up on the internet? No? Well, I interned at the *Cleveland Plain-Dealer* while I was finishing my degree at Western Reserve. They hired me after graduation. I stayed there for a while, then I moved to Detroit and went to work on the *Motor City Examiner*. I left there and ended up working at the *Pittsburgh Press*. After a number of years, I left *The Press*. Stayed in the 'burgh, though, and went to work for Richard Scaife at the *Tribune-Review*. Then after a while, for the rag of the same name here in Sutersberg.

"You don't have to ask your next question, I can see it on your face: Why did I leave so many places, did I quit or was I fired? Without going into the sordid details of each case, in some I left on my own and in others I was asked to leave. Seems I have issues of my own, Agent Plunkett. How's that for a successful career? I was at the end of my rope when I acquired the *Weekly Wise Shopper*. Got it for a song, as the saying goes. Actually, I got it for less than that. The previous owner literally gave it away. Or, I guess I should say, the bank gave it away. I couldn't have afforded it if they'd asked anything much for it. Everybody told me I was nuts to even consider taking a business that was already circling the porcelain, even though all I had to do was sign a paper at the bank.

"Oh, they were right, of course they were. In no time I found myself circling the same porcelain as the previous guy. That is the case, or was, until the Harlequin came along."

"Things have been looking up lately?"

"Like gangbusters. It's as if the Gods of Journalism have decided to bless me with success to make up for all Their previous neglect. I can do no wrong lately. First, I decided to write a little eyewitness piece on the first bank job last December, then I had a brainstorm and called the perp the Harlequin. How in the world did I come up with that archaic word? Beats me. Anyway, instead of sending the piece to the *Trib*, which was my original intention, I decided to slap it on the front page of *The Shopper*. There'd never been a story of any kind on the front page of *The Shopper*, only the usual ads and crap. What happens? Local media, TV, radio talk shows, all that, they all picked up on the Harlequin, on the name Harry Samuels stuck on him. I got my personal fifteen minutes of fame, and what's more *The Shopper* is making a buck for a change. Who'd a thunk it."

"Who, indeed," Plunkett said. He glanced at his watch. Ten past ten a.m. He assumed Sparks would be at the Annex HQ by then. He got up from the bench—his shirt was stuck to his back with sweat. "I need to be on my way, Mr. Samuels. My partner will be wondering where I wandered off to."

"Call me Harry, Agent Plunkett. Everybody does. You get back to crime fighting and I'll get back to the shop, to check on Helen." Samuels grinned at Plunkett, a toothy, aggressive grin. "I hope nothing I said helps you catch the Harlequin. As the saying goes, I'm making hay while the sun shines."

He looked both ways to avoid the sparse traffic, waved to Plunkett and crossed the avenue.

Chapter 6

With his necktie folded neatly into a pocket of his suit coat and the coat slung over his shoulder, Ed Plunkett turned south on Pennsylvania Avenue toward the nearest cross street he could see; a sign post on the corner told him it was Third Street. Third looked to be an easy uphill walk, and if he had the street grid of Sutersberg figured correctly, it led directly to South Main at a point three blocks below the Courthouse and its Annex, his destination.

His gait, small easy steps, was that of a man who had recently survived a heart incident; no other way of walking made sense in that heat. And his mind was chewing on the conversation with Harry Samuels. Samuels had an alibi, the very best alibi a person could have—he was in the Hempfield *PNC Bank* when the perp walked in dressed as a clown; the employees and customers would have seen them in the same place at the same time, they could not be one and the same person. Other than that...the things he said...well, ordinarily Harry Samuels would be considered an A1 suspect.

Before he was out of sight of the library, Plunkett saw a woman—an older woman, the librarian he presumed—open the front door from the inside and step out onto the library's small front porch. She was a tiny pigeon of a woman with a pigeon's round-breasted figure and dark hair peppered with gray. The librarian's wide mouth turned down when she surveyed the stoop and sidewalks in front of her domain and discovered no readers waiting impatiently to enter. Only one man was visible to her, Plunkett, and he was walking away. She waved and called out to him, "If you require a cooling off, sir, we are air conditioned."

He returned the wave with a nod but without stopping.

* * *

Wally Thorne, the decorated war hero of Operation Desert Storm, and his friend Socrates Barbonus, known to Pizza Countians as the little professor because of his tendency to run on about everything, were on their way to spend the rest of their day as usual in the Public Library when they encountered FBI Agent Plunkett cautiously walking up Third Street.

Thorne and Barbonus looked like homeless men to the FBI man and he was correct, they were homeless men, sort of. They looked and smelled the part, and they slept each night under the bandstand in St. Clair Park. Still, they were a welcome part of the local color, and as much at home as any two people could be in Sutersberg or anywhere else in Pizza County.

They had just concluded their daily breakfasts on the loading dock behind *Lucky Jack's Supermarket* located conveniently nearby at the foot of South Main Street hill. Their repasts consisted of bottomless tin mugs of coffee and not-too-stale items of yesterday's baked goods. Their host was grocer Kevin Winocher, son of the late Lucky Jack Winocher, who had recently passed and who had years ago started the tradition of free breakfasts on the loading dock for these two homeless guys. Son Kevin had taken over the management of the popular market from his father, but Kevin is not referred to as Lucky Kevin because when it comes to the management of a grocery store, everyone agreed the son was not the father. But like his father, Kevin had a good heart, so breakfast was still available free of charge every morning for Wally and the little professor.

The encounter on Third Street between the two homeless men and the FBI man was not much of an encounter, at least not from Ed Plunkett's perspective. He, having just abandoned the bench in front of the library, was strolling unhurriedly up Third, tie off and suit coat carried over one shoulder; the two homeless men were on the same side of the street coming down Third, having just returned from breakfast behind *Lucky Jack's Market*, the ex-soldier setting a long-legged pace and with the little professor scurrying to keep up while continuing to run on about something.

Suddenly sighting an approaching stranger and ID-ing him as a weapons-carrier, the ex-soldier's behavior became exaggerated: at first merely alert and on guard; next jumpy, bobbing, weaving as if he were dodging incoming rounds; then verging on out of control—it took all of the goateed little guy's physical strength and powers of persuasion to control his friend. To Agent Plunkett the situation was not quite tending toward dangerous, but still his hand instinctively went to the butt of the service weapon holstered at his waist.

Just as suddenly, as if a stiff wind had suddenly changed direction, the encounter was over: the little guy coaxed and cajoled his friend to cross to the other side of the street, and they continued on down the street and out of sight on Pennsylvania Avenue toward the front of the library. Plunkett shook his head and continued on up toward South Main.

Vehicular traffic had increased dramatically, especially truck traffic, as the morning was now well along. Employee activity could be heard from inside the U.S. Post Office as Plunkett passed it, but no patrons were in sight. Across South Main, a group of men were staring in the front window of the *Consumer Discount Company*; Plunkett could not imagine what the attraction was in the window of a loan company. Why there and not next door at *Cloris's Pretty Posie Shop*? The

FBI man was tempted to cross the street to see what was on display in the flower shop window—lately he seemed to get real pleasure from looking at and smelling flowers. Lately. Since he took one in the stomach. But the amount of diesel pollution from trucks trundling and belching up and down Main Street hill made breathing difficult and unpleasant. There was no pleasure to be had by lingering on Main Street.

The distance between Third and Second Streets was not great; Plunkett estimated it to be no more than fifty yards, give or take. But the entire space was taken up by a single building, a regal rectangle of crème-colored brick—the Gunderman Building. It formerly housed *Gunderman's Department Store*, the largest retail establishment in Pizza County. At present its innards were partitioned and rented as office space. Old Man Gunderman would roll over in his grave were he to see the building in its present state; his widow probably would, too. The Gundermans were long dead. Plunkett didn't know that, though he suspected it. It was clear to him as he strolled around Sutersberg that all of the downtown was a shadow of its former self.

Plunkett crossed Second Street and sauntered past the *PNC Bank* branch doing business on the ground level of the Levy Building. He picked up his pace when up ahead he spotted a neon sign for a workingman's clothing store. His curiosity was peaked: who was the 21st century workingman, really? What did he look like and what did he wear? Plunkett hoped looking in that store's window would answer those questions. However, before he had a chance to find out, a man who Plunkett immediately recognized exited the Courthouse and shambled into view. Even from a distance, the man was so remarkably and intentionally Lincoln-esque in manner and appearance that it had to be the District Attorney of Pizza County, John Grimes. The FBI man postponed his research on the 21st century workingman and stepped up his pace toward the DA.

Throughout a long career in the FBI, Jack Sparks, Ed Plunkett's boss and partner, had worked a number of cases in Pizza County; enough cases that he had become familiar with some of the County characters. He had sketched them out for Plunkett. Each meeting Plunkett had with one of those characters proved just how good a judge of them Sparks had been. Evidence of that: his description of District Attorney Grimes was right on the money. Sparks told Plunkett that John Grimes was an Honest Abe look-alike, a tall and wiry man with a long, homely face that only a mother could love. He looked and acted the part of a country bumpkin.

"But be careful with DA Grimes," Sparks had warned. "Not that you need to fear him in any way, we're on the same side of the law, after all. No, it's just that you have to be careful not to fall for that hayseed routine he puts on. John Grimes is no hayseed. He's a helluva good prosecutor and as sly a politician as you'll find anywhere."

Plunkett followed with his eyes as Grimes strutted along as if the sunny sidewalk were the runway at the County Fair. He waved to acquaintances in passing vehicles, got honks in reply, stopped to greet a woman walking with a child in hand; he had a few words for the woman, played got-your-nose with the child. Grimes was wearing his suit coat despite the heat, one of the custom-tailored suits for which Grimes was famous, with the trouser length a mite short to intentionally show white socks. The DA turned immediately toward the federal agent as soon as he spotted him. Approaching with a hand extended to be shaken, he said, "Wait, you don't have t' introduce yerself, I never forget a name or a face. Puckett, right? Agent Puckett, FBI?"

"You get points for being close, Mr. Grimes. It's Plunkett, Ed Plunkett. You got the FBI part right, though."

"Close is only good playing horseshoes, Ed. My apologies. I was just up to your HQ in the Annex. Figured I'd get me an update on the Harlequin pursuit. Hah." Clearly the DA was skeptical, as skeptical as Plunkett had to admit he was, himself.

"I don't hold much store with committees, Ed. I...you don't mind my calling you Ed? Right. I sent my best assistant DA in Marge Bash and I'm sure the other agencies have sent their best personnel to the task force, too." A skeptical look from Grimes. "But the way I see it, too many experts in one place and they just start getting' in each other's way, start tripping over each other's feet. Know what I mean?"

"We feel pretty much the same way, sir. I can assure you, the Bureau didn't want a task force, but the Governor..."

Grimes grimaced. "A Republican, 'nuf said. But maybe you'll get lucky. Somebody better get lucky or else prove me wrong about committees. This Harlequin son of a bitch is making us look bad. Real bad. We gotta put an end to him." He spotted a black ant scurrying across the concrete; he followed it, tromped on it. "At first he was fun, along with Christmas and New Year holidays. Pizza County made the papers with its own outlaw, sorta put us on the map, so to speak. What county wouldn't want its own outlaw, like Robin Hood or Zorro. Y'know? But later you realize the citizens are laughing their asses off at us elected officials for not being able to apprehend their outlaw. They start wonderin,' who they oughta vote for next election. Get my drift?"

"I do, yes sir, I do." Plunkett was thinking his partner was probably wondering where he was. He said, "You were saying before, you went to our HQ for an update. Was anything new this morning?"

Grimes shook his head. "Took me all of two seconds to be brought up to speed, just long enough for…Sparks, is it? Your partner…your boss?"

"Both, actually."

"Took Sparks no more than two seconds to tell me nothing was new. He was wondering where you were. They're waitin' on you before heading out to Millton to re-interview the bank employees. Official statements and all that. Fer all the good that'll do."

"Well, let's try and not be too skeptical, sir," Plunkett said, even though he was as much so as Grimes, if not more. If there were an FBI handbook, Plunkett felt as if he were quoting from the first page: "We never know what good will come from something we do. We turn over every rock, every single one no matter how small, in hope that something will turn up of value to our investigation. Eventually… who knows?"

Leaving that to hang in the hot, diesel-polluted air, Plunkett shook hands with DA Grimes and headed for the purer, frigid air of the Annex.

Chapter 7

Millton sits at the foot of the Laurel Mountains in an expansive valley that, despite the absence of a major waterway to transport heavy goods, had once been a hive of heavy industrial activity—coal mining, steel fabrication, beer brewing. Had once been. Most of that activity was in the past. Millton had other things to boast of now: for one, the prowess on the golf course of one of its bygone native sons; for another, Milltoners boasted having the regional hub, the *County Airport*, on its eastern outskirt. Millton was a bustling, charming little town according to what Ed Plunkett had been told; he had yet to see it for himself.

A part of the task force was on location in Millton: they, a group that included Agent Plunkett and his partner, Jack Sparks, along with Dom Ianuzzi, Chief of the Sutersberg cops and, of course, wherever his Chief went Poke Perkins went, so Poke was there, too. They, in the company of Fred Armbrust, Chief of the Millton cops, were at the site of the Harlequin's holdup the previous night, the *VitaBank* in the shopping center across Route 30 from the airport. For lack of other available breathing room, they were all squeezed into a circle around the head teller's desk in her glass cubicle of an office.

Agent Sparks had expressed his doubts about conducting interviews in the presence of the local cops. According to him, the locals were relative amateurs at working major crimes so they tended, in his words, "to fuck up the interviews by turning them into interrogations." They tended to shut down witnesses by setting a belligerent tone, thereby losing vital information. For instance, Sparks harbored particular doubts about Chief Ianuzzi, knowing that Nuzzi's mouth was as big as his ego, and his ego was as huge as his belly. As it turned out, both Ianuzzi and the local chief, Armbrust, stood as far back from the proceedings as available space permitted and surrendered the lead to the two federal agents.

Not that it turned out to matter, not that they learned much of anything new or brought anything to light that hadn't already been there. The first of three witnesses—two employees and a customer—was an Asian-American woman employee in her late twenties, very attractive—Damn! Plunkett thought when he spotted a wedding ring on the finger of her left hand, a hand carved of ivory with a pianist's long fingers. She had long, jet black hair and perfectly shaped, jade-colored almond eyes. At the moment, those eyes struggled to remain open. The woman's physician had insisted on giving her a dose of something for her nerves. Instead of calming her, it had turned her into a zombie. She kept falling asleep in the middle of sentences. They'd have to interview her again when the sedative wore off. Chief Armbrust sent her home with one of his cops.

The other employee at the scene, Myrna Tample, was the teller/manager of the Latrobe branch. She made a point of the fact that it was her desk they were gathered around. She said it not only with pride but with determination—she was prepared to defend her position if anyone of the men around her dared attempt to take it from her. Not one of them cared to try.

Plunkett recalled his ex-wife, whose name was Gail—he referred to her as The Gale— used to refer to women built like Myrna Tample as Size eighteens. Plunkett thought of Tample as a linebacker. She was a blonde though not a natural one; she looked as if she spent a lot of time and money in a beauty salon. A waste of time and money, she was not an attractive woman. Her skin was pale, as if she had had a recent fright, but she didn't look the type to be scared easily, and the skin of her face was the smoothest Plunkett had ever seen. Like a baby's ass, he thought.

He always had difficulty gauging people's ages, but still. Myrna Tample couldn't possibly be old enough to have worked for the *VitaBank Corporation* for as many years as she claimed. He turned away and was about to whisper this concern to his partner, when Sparks, way ahead of him, mumbled, "Botox treatments, Ed."

Ms Tample didn't wait to be asked a question, but just started talking; she was a contralto. "We were busy as bees, Sue Lee and I, at the drive-up windows. They're ninety percent of our business, the drive-up windows, especially on Friday afternoons. Hardly anybody comes inside the building, even on hot summer days. Which it was, a hot one yesterday. Like today and like tomorrow, if you believe the weatherman..."

Get on with it, Plunkett thought. Enough with the weather report. The A/C was failing to keep the crowded office cool, Myrna Tample's contralto voice was grating on his nerves, and he had to pee.

"In our positions at the drive-up counter, our backs are to the front entry door; when I heard the door chime, I glanced at the clock. It was 3:47 p.m. I didn't even turn around to see who it was, I assumed it was Mr. Kronzek from the hardware store across the way. He comes in to make his daily deposit at approximately that time every weekday. Mostly checks, not much cash in his establishment anymore. Not much cash in most retail establishments anymore. Changing times, eh, gentlemen? Anyway, I assumed it was Mr. Kronzek but then I realized the door had chimed twice. Did Mr. Kronzek leave for some reason, or did someone else come in? Were there now two customers in the bank or was there only one? Immediately I turned to see. That's when I found the Harlequin at my..."

Sparks interrupted, "You don't mean the Harlequin, you mean Richard Nixon, right?"

"Yes, correct. Richard Nixon." She fell silent, but she led belligerently with her chin. She didn't like to be interrupted.

Plunkett stepped in. "Go on please, Ms Tample."

"All right. He, Richard Nixon, if you will," she said, glaring at Sparks, "He said, 'I'm not a crook, but if you don't mind, I'll make a withdrawal.' He said that and stepped back to threaten with whatever he had in his jacket pocket. You know, as if he had a gun. Maybe it was a gun, maybe not. I couldn't tell."

"Well, what happened next?"

"What happened next was, I hissed at him."

No interruptions this time. Both federal agents were flummoxed. "You what-ed at him?"

"I hissed at him like he was a stray cat, which if you ask me is just what he is. I made it quite clear that he was going to get no money from Myrna Tample." Her chest inflated with pride.

"And...?" Plunkett prompted.

"And he shrugged, turned and went out the door."

"Now wait," Sparks was interrupting again. "Do I understand you to mean that he left, walked out, empty handed?"

"You understand me perfectly. He turned, made a big V with his arms, like you see in all the TV news stories about him, did it right in front of Mr. Kronzek, who looked as if his feet were frozen to the floor, poor man, and went right out the door."

Plunkett wanted to ask Ms. Tample, He had a gun, didn't he? At least he might've had one. Weren't you afraid? But he couldn't wait any longer, the slug he took in the gut had nicked a kidney and ever since then.... He asked her instead, "Ma'am, Is there a restroom? I need to...uh, wash up."

David Kronzek, owner/operator of *Kronzek's Hardware*, was dressed for the weather: shorts, a white tee shirt and white NB shoes without socks. What little was left of his hair was light brown, shaved close all around his head. Plunkett judged him to be pushing sixty. Two things struck Plunkett about him: first, his were the kind of hairy legs with spavined knees that caused most men to avoid wearing shorts, yet there his legs were unashamedly in full view; also, either he suffered Parkinson's disease, or he had been badly frightened by the Harlequin and was making no attempt to cover the fact. He was still trembling. He could use a dose of what the Doc had given the other teller, the one Ms Tample referred to as Sue Lee.

Without making reference to Ms Tample's comment that yesterday afternoon he, Kronzek, had appeared to be frozen in fear, Sparks asked him if the Harlequin had frightened him. Kronzek admitted as much.

He said, "I didn't have any cash on me. I had a five-dollar bill in my pocket to treat myself to one of those Beano Frappuccinos they make at the *Viva Mexicale Coffee Bar*. I think they mix baked beans in with the coffee beans to make them, y' know. Man, do they pack a wallop. Sorry, uh, I tend to rattle on when I'm nervous. Yeah. The fiver was all I had, oh, and the checks for my daily deposit. Of course."

Plunkett asked, "You take personal checks at your store? You're not afraid you might get stung with bad paper?"

Kronzek gawked at the FBI man. "In Millton?"

"So you weren't afraid of being robbed, you didn't have anything. Then what scared you, if you don't mind my asking?"

"I heard, when you get held up and you don't have anything worth taking, the robber gets angry, turns violent. I heard that or read it somewheres. The internet, maybe. That worried me, but that guy, the Harlequin, seemed like a really nice guy. Still, he was standing right next to me, and he had a gun. Was I scared? Damn right. I got three kids."

When asked if he could describe the gun, Kronzek admitted that he didn't actually see the gun or any other weapon. He assumed the Harlequin had one in his jacket pocket.

And how did he know the Harlequin was a nice, polite guy? Kronzek replied, "He offered to let me go ahead of him in the teller line." That surprised the federal agents. Kronzek added, "I didn't take him up on the offer."

Chapter 8

"Hang a left out of the Shopping Center and keep going east." So they had been directed by Millton Chief Armbrust: "It's only a hundred yards or so, but go damn slow or you'll miss it, sure as hell." The Chief was referring to the *Gridiron Club*. "The best spot in Millton to git you a good meal and a brewski or two."

Nominally a private club, so it was out of the jurisdiction of the State Liquor Control authorities. The *Gridiron Club* had been there on Route 30 outside of Millton in one form or another for two centuries, claiming itself and Millton as being the legitimate founding home of professional football. The FBI men hadn't searched for signage visible from the road announcing the Club's presence because they were told there wasn't any.

"It's kinda like this," quoted Chief Armbrust to sum up the *Gridiron Club* members' attitudes: "If you don't already know where it is, you prob'ly don't belong there." Maybe Sparks and Plunkett didn't belong there, but the FBI men were there as guests of the Millton Chief of Police, who was a member and who had called ahead to insure the two feds were served.

Beyond a vast parking lot that it shared with a bowling alley, the *Gridiron Club* was an unassuming, one-story building of soot-stained red brick. Inside, the owner or owners' taste in décor ran to shellacked, knotted pine board paneling, both in the barroom and the main dining room. The bar seated eight patrons on round, plastic-covered stools with a few two-fer tables fitted in along the far wall. The knotted pine walls of the separate and much larger dining room were decorated with framed photos and amateurish, painted portraits of footballers from the fifties and earlier.

Sparks and Plunkett were seated at a table in the main dining room enjoying the first bites of the Club's juicy Steakburgers. It was quiet enough at the late lunch hour that they were able to eavesdrop on an adjacent table, where a foursome of middle-aged women dressed for golf were telling each other lies, the FBI men were sure; they were rehashing every stroke of the nine holes they had just finished at a nearby golf links. The Federal agents found the ladies' chatter calming and amusing. They would have found chatter on any subject except the exploits of the Harlequin calming and amusing, although it was impossible to avoid the subject in their own conversation.

Plunkett sank his teeth into one of the largest, juiciest cheeseburgers he'd ever bitten into—a blob of ketchup oozed out of the bun onto his chin. He used a paper napkin to wipe himself.

He said, referring to Millton Chief Armbrust, "What's to be gained by blaming the local cops for sloppy police work, Jack? You've said it yourself a million times, 'Sloppy work is the only kind they know. At least Armbrust was right about the food in this place. Best burger I ever ate, bar none. Give him credit for that, at least."

Sparks speared a piece of open-faced steak sandwich with his fork. He chewed vigorously, looking as if he wanted to chew Chief Armbrust. He spoke around a half-full mouth, "Imagine that bum keeping quiet the fact that the Harlequin left the bank empty handed? Without a red cent. Jeez." He chewed some more. "His explanation? Nobody asked him. Jeez."

Talk about sloppy work, Plunkett thought. We, for one, didn't ask, either did we? He thought it but decided not to mention it. Instead, "Have you tried these French fries, Jack? Man. Mickey Ds can't touch them." He dipped one in ketchup and popped it into his mouth. "You know what I would ask the Harlequin if he were sitting here right now? I'd ask, 'What in the world are you up to with these bank jobs? They're federal crimes, for chrissake, with heavy penalties. Years in prison. You know we're gonna catch you eventually, even if it takes forever, you know damn well we will. It's inevitable. Why, for so little money? It's not worth it, so c'mon, what are you up to?' That's what I would ask if he were here."

Sparks said, "Too bad he's not, I wouldn't mind hearing his answer." They both busied themselves chewing. Sparks signaled the server for two more IC Lites.

"Maybe he's smarter than we think. Chief Armbrust, I mean. Maybe he didn't want the media to find out no cash was taken from the bank. By not telling us he kept it from them, as well. He's right thinking they'd make a big deal out of it, if they learned it. They'd make an even bigger deal if they learned of that guy Kronzek's statement that the Harlequin was a nice, polite guy. You can bet your ass on that. But as of this morning's edition of the *Trib*, the media folks don't know either thing yet." He took a bite of the dill pickle that came alongside his burger. Then, "I'm thinking maybe Armbrust isn't so dumb, Jack."

Sparks pulled at his beer; he shook his head. "You're giving him a lotta credit, I'm not so sure. Anyhow, for your information, I saw that guy you interviewed this morning…Samuels? I saw him and Armbrust with their heads together after last night's press conference. Who knows what questions were asked and what Armbrust answered? Anybody's guess."

Harry Samuels, Plunkett thought, who admitted he hoped we wouldn't catch the Harlequin. Of course he hoped we wouldn't, The *Wise Shopper* was making money for a change.

He said, "Yeah, Harry Samuels. Typical media guy. They want it all from you but ask them for something and they clam up tight. He never said a word to me about his talking to Chief Armbrust. All he told me was that he hadn't written the article for the front page of the *Wise Shopper* yet. Said he never writes it till he works himself up into the right frame of mind. Y'know? The mockingly satirical frame of mind."

Plunkett shook off his dislike of journalists with a shake of the head. He raised his brewski in tribute. "Here's to another scoop for old Hairy S."

Chapter 9

Ask any born-and-bred western Pennsylvanian and they will tell you: If you don't like the weather just be patient for fifteen minutes and it'll change. You may not like the change, probably not, but be certain, it will change.

The fifteen minutes was an exaggeration, of course, but Ed Plunkett, born-and-bred to the bone Pittsburgher that he was, was not surprised when he and his boss stepped beyond the front door of the *Gridiron Club* to find a change in the weather. The wind was kicking up, and he noticed it had also changed direction, coming now from the north. In addition to the wind changes, the sun seemed to have lost its sting as its rays had to sift through a veil of thin, gray clouds. The humidity had fallen way off, as well. The agents breathed sighs of relief.

For the first time since their departure from Pittsburgh, Sparks took the wheel for the ten-mile drive back from Millton to Sutersberg. Plunkett was surprised to discover that his partner and immediate superior was a cautious driver, sticking to the right-hand lane and the posted fifty-five mph speed limit. When the first droplets of rain pattered on the windshield, he slowed their vehicle to fifty mph.

Plunkett said, "Bless the weatherman, I believe he overheard my prayers. This rain'll cool things off, make it easier to breathe."

Sparks looked over at his passenger reluctantly, not comfortable taking his eyes off the road. He risked it, though. He said, "Having trouble breathing, Ed?" He announced his intention to drop Plunkett off at their motel. "I'm taking you back to the motel. No arguments, Ed. I haven't forgotten you're supposed to be on limited duty. You look pooped. You look like you could use a nap. Nothing for us to do at the moment, anyhow, except wait around the Annex for Forensics to submit their report on last night's…incident. I won't be needing a hand, just sitting around waiting. I can do that myself."

No point or sense in arguing with Sparks, his mind was obviously made up. And to be honest, Plunkett agreed about his needing a nap. Besides, he expected nothing but frustration from the forensics report. He ticked off the frustrations in his head:

The Harlequin chose his sites well, and his timing was perfect. There were too many branch banks in the Tri-County area; no one had enough manpower to watch them all. And there were never many witnesses.

The Harlequin never touched anything, so no fingerprints for identification.

He was never observed coming to a branch or going from one; no vehicle to associate with him.

He always managed to create an atmosphere of unreality or make believe that seemed to paralyze witnesses into cooperating with him; his appearances seem conjured, theatrical.

No, there would be nothing but frustration unless or until the Harlequin made a mistake. Meanwhile, a nap sounded divine.

Chapter 10

The Federal budget for the Harlequin Task Force (as revised) included the cost of two rooms at the *Executive Motor Inn*, the oldest, twice remodeled motel on the eastern outskirt of Sutersberg. The original unrevised budget accounted for only one room, but Ed Plunkett told the boss, A.I.C. Alan Bluestone, that since being gut shot his sleep was...troubled, to say the least, and he was afraid his nightly moaning and prowling would disturb his partner, prevent Sparks from getting his badly needed rest. Bluestone, considering the efficiency of the force to be at risk, saw to it that the budget was revised.

Ed Plunkett was in favor of camaraderie and all that rah rah team bullshit, but he found it a relief to have his own room. And he hadn't exaggerated in order to get it, his sleep was indeed...troubled, as he had put it to Bluestone, without further explanation. He didn't tell Bluestone or anyone else about the nightmares. About having to take a nine-mm slug in the gut each and every night in the most vivid and excruciating detail. Ed needed rest as much as any man, but lately he tended to dread sleeping.

His motel room was no great shakes as an accommodation: it was a twenty-by-fifteen-foot rectangle, with a bathroom/shower combination toward the far end, twin double beds toward the front opposite the door, a small flat screen TV mounted on top of a chest of drawers opposite the beds. Window-mounted A/C. No great shakes, for sure, but it was clean, and it was his alone.

Plunkett was in his shorts and a tee shirt in one of the two beds, a cover sheet and threadbare blanket pulled up as far as his waist. He faced the TV, his back propped against the headboard, which was bolted to the wall. Fending off sleep, successfully so far, but…

First Leno and the late show, then an old Schwarzenegger action flick, then a late late… His neck ached from the effort of holding up his head. Getting drowsy...

Before he was aware of having moved, Agent Plunkett found himself in a dark, abandoned warehouse. He, along with two other agents wearing Kevlar vests under windbreakers with FBI on the backs, were confronted by two surly men—big armed men. And a teenage boy, rather puny in size but with a huge cannon in his hand. "FBI," one of the agents yells, "Drop your weapons and hands on your heads." The two big bad guys comply, but the kid stands frozen in place, staring at Plunkett with the roundest, loneliest brown eyes Ed had ever seen. It were as if Plunkett could peer deep into those eyes and see his future there. "Don't," he said to the kid. "Don't," but the kid did.

Bang! Oh…Plunkett grabbed at his stomach as he folded to the greasy warehouse floor. Pain!!

Plunkett awoke in a sweat, his belly aching and the sound of gunfire echoing in his ears.

Chapter 11

On a drizzling Thursday morning, Chief Dominic Ianuzzi hurried out of *Dunkin' Donuts*, located by intention a stone's throw from the Sutersberg Police Station; he hustled past the station, continuing north on Main Street. He wore a black, weatherproof windbreaker with Police on the back over his uniform blouse and a plastic cover on his uniform cap. In hand he carried several of the latest issues of the *Weekly Wise Shopper* that he impounded from the pile at the entrance to *Lucky Jack's Supermarket*. Once inside the Courthouse Annex, he began distributing the fliers to everyone he encountered. The object of interest and ridicule was, of course, Harry Samuels's editorial on the front page. As usual it was the only text beside ads and cents-off coupons in the pamphlet-sized handout. The banner headline demanded attention:

THE HARLEQUIN STRIKES AGAIN

The infamous Piazza County Harlequin, in another of his many mysterious appearances Friday in the late afternoon, entered and robbed the drive-up branch of *VitaBank* in the Millton Shopping Center across Route 30 from the County Airport. This time the Harlequin was disguised as former President Richard M. Nixon.

The Harlequin insisted that he was not a crook, just as President Nixon, himself, had done, but then proceeded to relieve the tellers of an as yet unknown amount of cash. As usual, no weapon was shown, and no threats were made. One bank employee, who wished to remain anonymous, told this reporter that the Harlequin's behavior was at all times mannerly and chivalrous toward the bank employees, all females.

One has to wonder—this reporter does, anyway—at the inability to apprehend this audacious criminal. Are WE THE PEOPLE of Piazza County bearing witness to genius on the part of the Harlequin? Or is it negligence and incompetence on the part of law enforcement and our elected officials?

For the *Weekly Wise Shopper*

Harry Samuels, editor-in-chief

Chapter 12

Once again, ask any western Pennsylvanian and they will tell you—they will, especially if you ask the same ones you asked before: You don't like the weather so you wait fifteen minutes and it does change, but you don't like the change. Will the changed weather hang around long? Or will it change back if you decide to wait another fifteen minutes? The answer is: Suck it up, brother, because bad weather tends to hang around forever. In western Pennsylvania it does.

The Rain Gods who ruled the skies over Pizza County have been hard at work since that week ago Thursday afternoon; it has rained cats and dogs since then. Although it was only drizzling at the moment, every once in a while, a distant rumble of thunder could be heard, an indication of a change for the worse, from cats and dogs to buckets.

The threat of impending worse weather has discouraged most foot and vehicular traffic. The Harlequin loved Pizza County, the place and the people—he really did—and he disliked thinking ill of them, but they were sissies when it came to precipitation, any form of precipitation. They hated rain, snow, sleet, hail; hated them all equally. The way they cowered indoors... The way they complained...

Never mind, he thought, it was glorious weather for a bank robbery. Parked a discreet distance from the *Greenbelt Federal Credit Union*, he scanned the entire strip of storefronts through the rain-spattered windshield of his car.

The village of Greenbelt. Simple, single-story houses in neat rows built before World War II; a pizza shop and a convenience store; a small factory for the production of sport coats and winter jackets; a pair of side-by-side garages converted to a municipal building; a Federal Credit Union building with a parking lot and drive-up window on one side.

It was doubtful Greenbelt's population totaled two hundred unless you counted domesticated animals as well as people. It was founded in the 1930s using funds from a then-new Federal Subsistence Homesteading program. It was one of the many pet projects of the famous wife of an American president who paid a well-publicized visit there in 1937. The socialistic ideal of the program, like many other programs created in Washington D.C. during the Great Depression, was to aid displaced industrial workers, rural farmers and poor coal miners, to help them relieve or eliminate the stresses and strains caused by capitalism. The Harlequin was no socialist, but he did intend to help Greenbelt eliminate the stresses and strains of capitalism. By robbing the Credit Union.

Flipping up the hood of his rainproof jacket against the drizzle, he climbed out of the car and unlocked the trunk. He transferred two items to the front passenger seat: a metal fisherman's tackle box that he'd converted to a makeup kit, and a cardboard carton that contained bits of props, costumes and disguises. Back behind the wheel, he rummaged among gauzy strands of fake hair, pads of paint and gummy bottles. He found a white hairpiece and tugged it into place on his bald head. Not a bad fit, he saw in the rearview mirror. "Ha-ha." Next he painted spirit gum on his upper lip and chin—Hold on a minute, let it get tacky—and pressed against the gum a white mustache and goatee, followed by another inspection in the rearview mirror. Colonel Sanders peered back at him. He couldn't restrain a giggle. "We do chicken right," he declared aloud. "Hee-hee."

Get hold of yourself.

He scanned once more for pedestrians. None. He returned the makeup kit and carton of disguises to the trunk and removed an empty cardboard tub that once contained twenty pieces of extra crispy chicken. He admired his likeness on the side of the carton. The Harlequin walked toward the entrance of the Credit Union, his usual purposeful stride giving way to the rolling, swaggering gait of an elderly Kentucky Colonel.

One last peek through the bank's glass door for good measure. "Ha-ha." Perfect. No customers and only one teller working.

He pushed his way inside. Swaggered up to the teller's window and placed the chicken bucket on the counter. The teller was a twenty-something woman with tweezed eyebrows, a tattoo of a red rose on one forearm, and a youthful grin on a heavily made-up face. A bright white toothy grin. Amused by his costume. Good.

"Mawnin, mah deah," the Harlequin drawled. He almost broke into another giggle; he was so pleased with the accent. "Ah'd be much obliged if y'all would fill up this heah bucket, and ah doan mean wif eleven herbs an' spices. Be quick, now, and I'll be gone."

The teller did as she was told, with never a crack in the youthful grin. With bucket under one arm, he backed away from the teller's window and in a courtly manner, bowed to her.

"Ah thank y'all, ma'am. Yes'm, ah do indeed." And swaggered out the door. A quick look around. "Ha-ha." No one. He swaggered to his car. Gingerly peeling the false whiskers from his face with one hand, he steered the car out of the parking lot.

Chapter 13

A rapid series of knocks on the front door startled Helen Waugaman out of her open-mouthed, trance-like stare at the computer screen. She pushed the magnifying readers up off her ski jump of a nose and gawked at the unexpected person who was blocking the open doorway and looking around the office with a controlled but slightly horrified look on her face. Helen was more than a little nearsighted, so whoever was standing in the doorway was something of a blur, but if she weren't mistaken the blur represented either a pre-teen girl or a very short woman with a wild bush of curly red, no, orange hair. Or was it an orange beret? No, hair. The blur was shaking its head, no and no. It was lost, obviously.

Helen left her composing seat. As she approached the blurred object at the door, she thought her initial guess was correct that the blur was a girl, not a woman; a girl with round green eyes as well as an orange, afro-shaped hairdo. There was something familiar about this girl. Helen was thinking she had seen this child, this girl, this lost young waif somewhere before. Waif? Where did that word come from? Yes, of course, waif was the kind of word Harry would use. It sounded old, that word, but it sure did fit. She'd seen her somewhere before. But where?

"I'm looking for..." The waif checked a page in a pocket-sized notebook she retrieved from her purse. "...for a Mr. Harry Samuels?"

"You're lettin' the flies in," Helen said.

"It says it right here….," the young woman said, referring to the notebook again. *The Weekly Wise Shopper*. 112 South Pennsylvania Avenue. Sutersberg. That's here, right?" Still shaking her head, the green eyes filled with hope that it was not right.

"Sorry," Helen apologized without knowing why. Still wondering where she had seen this waif before.

"Professor Terwelliger assured me, If I mentioned his, Professor Terwelliger's name, he was sure Mr. Samuels would grant me an interview. He told me, too. I'd find Mr. Samuels here." Again pointing to her little notebook.

"Perfessor who?"

"Terwelliger. Professor Scott Terwelliger of Grove City College School of Journalism."

Helen shook her head. "Heard of Perfessor Barbonus. Never heard of a Perfessor Ter…whatever."

"Well, Mr. Samuels must have. Professor Terwelliger told me they used to work together, him and Mr. Samuels. For The… I don't know, some Pittsburgh newspaper I never heard of. Is he here, is Mr. Samuels here? If he is…." The orange-haired waif examined the room, taking in the posters and old newspaper clippings taped to the walls, the two battered desks, the counter with its walk-through flap at one end that separated the reception area from the work area. Under her breath she said, "If he's here, why am I?" Hoping while asking for Mr. Samuels that there was no good reason for his being there, and hoping she was right.

Where in hell was Harry Samuels? That's what she would like to know. After iterating and re-iterating that her department head at Grove City College had assured her that a mere mention of his name would be all the intro she would need to be granted an interview with Harry Samuels, and after Helen Waugaman—not prone to much in the way of conversation to begin with—had iterated and re-iterated that Harry wasn't there, the neophyte journalist had decided to revert to her original instinct, which was to flee the premises of *The Weekly Wise Shopper* and hunt for Mr. Samuels elsewhere. But where?

She trudged the entire length of Main Street, south to north, in hopes of finding him, but without success.

She came upon a parklet and bench in a vacant lot beside the Gunderman Building; the bench was occupied by an obese woman who introduced herself as Melvina or was it Malverna? It was impossible to tell; having no teeth, her speech was garbled. Also at the bench was a blind man named Bill, who thrust an old fedora hat that contained unsharpened pencils at her. She donated a dollar in hope of getting information from the old derelict. What she got instead was Blind Bill's longstanding joke: "Harry Samuels? I haven't seen him." She left the two of them laughing.

She searched in every restaurant, café and diner along the way, without having a bite of lunch herself, in hope of finding him. Instead, she found what seemed like the entire legal profession in the *Iberian Tea Room*, the entire medical profession, those avoiding the hospital cafeteria, in *Salerno's Trattoria*, and the entire dental profession around the corner from Main at the *Elks Club* on Otterman Street. She even encountered two homeless men at Irene's Lunch Counter on the ground floor of the old Medical Building on Maple Avenue. To a man or woman, they all knew Harry but hadn't seen him.

She reached the top of Main Street hill, the chuffing and honking of traffic assaulting her ears, the occasional gust of wind kicking street grit into the air. She found The Catholic Cathedral, its rectory and the *Catholic Elementary School*, all named for Bishop Piazza, with the

Jewish *Temple Beth Israel* practically in its shadow, up there on one side of Main, and the *Sutersberg Public Elementary School* and the *Piazza County Museum of American Art* on the other. She didn't think there was any point in searching any of those places for Harry Samuels.

Hungry, tired and disappointed that she had to return empty-handed, she turned downhill, down Otterman Street to Pennsylvania, made a left past *Harvey's Hardware*—checking in there for Samuels. Nope—to return to the decrepit office of the *Weekly Wise Shopper*.

✳ ✳ ✳

Meanwhile the two FBI men, Sparks and Plunkett, were devouring the last slices of a special meat-lover's pizza at *Arcangelo's* in south Sutersberg, across the way from St. Bruno's R.C. Church. Again at the recommenddation of Police Chief Dominic Ianuzzi. Since federal agents were often obliged to work cases in unfamiliar territory, Assistant AIC Sparks had a rule he swore by: "Looking for a good place to eat? Ask the fattest guy in town." In this particular case, that was Chief Ianuzzi.

"Chief Armbrust was right about *The Gridiron Club* last week," Plunkett said. "And Nuzzi was right about this pizza!"

Sparks said, "If you can't get good pizza in Pizza County, where the hell can you!" He dropped a piece of pepperoni onto the table in front of him, retrieved it and popped it into his mouth. He said, "I'm sure you noticed right away, everybody around here calls it Pizza County, not Piazza County. It's been that way…I think, forever."

Well, maybe not forever. Back in the 1960s, Nuzzi told the FBI agents, so many dining establishments— restaurants, cafes, diners, lunch counters, food trucks—

had pizza on the menu and had "We serve Pizza" signs in the windows of their establishments, so many, as an example of how bad it had gotten, that Common Pleas Judge Leonard Olafsen hung a sign on the door of his courtroom,

We serve Justice Here and pizza.

So much pizza was baking in the County, in fact, it was reported that a pall of burning mozzarella cheese hung over Sutersberg like smog. If you were a child of the 1960s living here, you awoke each morning to the smell of burning mozzarella cheese and when bedtime rolled around you were still breathing in that aroma, as welcome and satisfying to you as your mother's good night kiss.

That was when one wiseacre from the senior class of Sutersberg Hi—no one knows for sure who it was. Many have claimed credit, including local dentist, Doc Goldenson—but whoever that wise guy was, he started the thing, started calling it Pizza County. A half century later, though the sobriquet stuck and everyone still calls it Pizza County, most of the pizza joints did not survive and the mozzarella smog is gone.

"When it comes to restaurants around here," Plunkett said, "Law enforcement can sure pick 'em."

Sparks replied, "Um, if only they were half as good at picking bank thieves. But I give them a little credit, they do seem to be trying. They think their jobs are on the line."

"You really think they're trying?"

"Yeah, I do, they're trying. They're hauling in for questioning every man in the County who has ever worn an orange jumpsuit. Every petty thief. Every man's ever been cited for spitting on the sidewalk has likely been hauled in by Nuzzi or Armbrust and given the third degree."

"Any results? Nothing?"

Sparks frowned and answered his colleague's hopeful glance with a shake of the head. "Nothing. Those people he's bringing in, they're not the kind of criminals we're used to dealing with. They're the victims of poverty, mostly, they're a bunch of numbnuts idiots too dumb to stay out of trouble. The Harlequin is not that kind, he's too smart. Look, we've been on the case for ...how long? Months? With what for our trouble? Not a clue, not a suspect, not a...nothing."

Plunkett was inclined to make light of their present situation, even though his job could be on the line, too. He just wasn't sure how his partner, who was showing frayed edges of frustration, would take it. He drew a slow breath and said, "You're making the Harlequin out to be a master criminal. If so, at this point in the novel Arthur Conan Doyle would have Inspector LaStrade show up at 221B Baker Street to consult with Sherlock Holmes." He breathed a little easier when he saw Sparks grin at the mention of the fictional master detective.

"No," Sparks said, "If this was a novel, the author would've given us a handful of likely suspects, and the detectives—that'd be us, Ed—would've been chasing red herrings all over three Counties. Well, where's our suspects? At this point I'd welcome a red herring or two, wouldn't you?"

"Actually...actually I thought I had one..." Plunkett said, "...when Harry Samuels told me he hoped we'd never catch the Harlequin. I grant, he's not much of a red herring, but at the time I thought, could it be him? Could he be the Harlequin? But nah, Harry Samuels couldn't be the Harlequin, not unless he was some kind of magician. He was in the bank...January, wasn't it? He was in the bank the same time the Harlequin was, so unless he was doing it with smoke and mirrors, like those magicians on TV..."

Plunkett thought of magicians and smoke and mirrors, knew it wasn't possible, yet he was reluctant to let go of the idea.

Sparks read disappointment on the face of his partner. He took a mouthful of his Mountain Dew, now mostly melted ice, and said, "Did Samuels say that? Did he say he was in the bank at the same time as the Harlequin? I looked at those articles he wrote on the front page of that shopping rag he runs. Several members of the taskforce, including Nuzzi, have saved all the back issues. I read them all. Well, not all, just the front pages. You should, too. We get back to the Annex, ask somebody to show you those back issues. I can tell you, Ed, he's kinda vague on details like where he was and where the Harlequin was. Maybe, after all, you might be right, he could be our first suspect."

"Yeah, maybe so," Plunkett replied, revived. "Or anyway our first red herring."

Chapter 14

After having been told once again that Mr. Samuels was not there, the young journalism student spun on her heels and stepped toward the door. At that moment the door flew open and Harry, too eager to escape the glaring midday heat to be paying attention to where he was going or what was in his path, and never ever expecting to encounter anyone in the *Wise Weekly Shopper* office, rushed in the door—bumper cars!

A moment after the collision: Harry, with a tiny smarmy grin on his usually expressionless face, thought, A man can learn a lot about a woman if he bumps into her at high speed. For one thing, she was indeed a woman. There was not much to her, weight- or height-wise, so she rebounded off him like a lively rubber ball. But not off him until he discovered the most substance of her was located under the oversized gray sweatshirt she was wearing. She successfully carried off a combination look of Little Orphan Annie and grunge, but under the sweatshirt she was all chests.

Unlike the girl at the moment of collision, Harry had not lost his balance and instinctively grabbed the young waif—without giving it a moment's thought he had put the word 'waif' on her—by the shoulders. Helen, as was her stolid way in all situations, hadn't moved from her place at the counter.

Harry called out, "Helen! I've been run over! Did you get the license number? It was a little orange sports car, I think. Ha-ha!"

He and the girl looked at each other and apologized, she for crashing into him, out of politeness even though she knew it had been the other way around; he for the joke, because she didn't seem to take it well.

Releasing the grip he had on her shoulders, Harry staggered to his desk and dropped into a creaking swivel chair. He drew a tissue from a box on the desk and used it to mop perspiration from his forehead. The action made him notice how much more hair had been replaced by forehead lately. Soon his forehead would reach all the way to the back of his head. With another tissue he cleaned the lenses of a pair of rimless glasses and placed them on his tiny, unassuming nose.

"Well, don't just stand there gaping," he said to Helen. "Introduce me to our guest, why don't you?" When it became apparent that Helen not only would not but could not introduce her, Harry looked at the girl and said, "Okay, we give up. Who are you?"

She replied that her name was EmmaGrace, all one word, EmmaGrace McManus, but that on the Grove City College campus, where she and other Journalism students staffed the *Grove City Collegian*, she went by E.G.

"It was Professor Scott Terwelliger's idea," she said. "That it would look great as a byline: E.G. McManus."

The idea may have originated with Scott Terwelliger, Harry mused, but just the thought of her name on a byline had set stars twinkling in those big green waif's eyes of hers.

Harry said, "How is my old pal Scottie Terwelliger? Haven't seen him or heard from him in an age. We worked on the same newspapers two…no, three different times, but we lost track of each other. After my last job in Ohio, The *Akron Beacon Journal*, I think it was, I came east, first to Pittsburgh then to Pizza County to work for Richard Scaife, and Scottie…well, I guess he went to Grove City."

She asked if he would grant her an interview. Harry replied that he was very busy at the moment—a splutter from Helen, who had retreated to the layout room—but…since she was one of Scott Terwelliger's Journalism students, he would make an exception. She came up with a yellow legal pad and pen from a bag she'd been holding.

Harry asked, "Should I call you EmmaGrace or do you prefer E.G.? E.G., I should have known. How about if I start with a brief bio, okay? Here goes."

And Harry went, as if he had rehearsed it.

"I was born in Erie, PA, but around age one my parents moved to Cleveland. So, I'm an Ohio boy through and through, a product of the Cleveland public school system and Ohio University in Athens, Ohio. That's where we met, Scottie Terwelliger and me, at Ohio U; we both worked on the school paper, *The Ohio University Post*. We did internships every summer, once on *The Athens Weekly* and two summers on *The Cleveland Plain Dealer*. They got to know us pretty well, there, at *The Plain Dealer*, so they hired us both after graduation."

EmmaGrace noticed how well rehearsed Harry's bio was; noticed too the intentional omission of dates.

"I stayed there in Cleveland for about three years. After that I worked for a time in Cincinnati, in Youngstown, back again in Akron, then to Pittsburgh to work on *The Trib*. That's *The Piazza County Tribune-Review*, Pittsburgh edition, and lastly for The Trib's local edition, out here."

"You moved around a lot." A simple statement by E.G., but it contained an implied, Why, that Harry recognized.

"I did, didn't I? I moved around a lot." Harry stalled, hoping for another more comfortable question, but E.G. stalled, too, waiting for him to answer the first one. Harry realized he needed to re-evaluate Scott Terwelliger's student. There was more to her in more ways than one, it seemed.

"Y'know, while I was moving around I never gave any thought to why I was doing it, I just did it. Thinking back on it now, though, I think I was just plain bored, bored with small town newspapers and small town minds. I needed something more and I went looking for it. Does that make sense to you? It seems right to me."

She put down the pad and pen, a move that Harry took as a warning. She looked right at him and said, "You expect me to believe all the moves you mentioned were your idea? I wasn't born yesterday, Mr. Samuels."

"A word of advice, E.G.," he said, with his voice sharp at the end. "I suppose that's why Scottie sent you to me, for advice? Well, here comes some: Don't start an interview by pissing off the interviewee. You'll get nothing that way. While it's true I didn't always agree with my so-called superiors, and sometimes I didn't show management the proper amount of respect, and I suppose a time or two my departure was by mutual consent..."

She thought as much and said so.

Harry was more than a little irked by her. He said, "I needed something more and I moved on to try to find it."

E.G. patted her orange afro hair behind her right ear, as if she felt it had come undone. Impossible for that Brillo pad to fall, Harry thought.

It was apparent to E.G. that her probing had pissed Samuels off, but she decided to risk a follow up anyway: "Like, what was the something you were looking for?

Did you know? What did you need that you didn't find?"

Harry decided to not answer that question, but she foiled him by just waiting through another awkward silence. He stared at the freckles beneath her green ovals of eyes and wanted to slap that pathetic waif's face of hers.

He snarled, "The big story—the Watergate, the 9-11, the assassination of MLK. You understand, dammit? The big one that gets your byline on page one above the fold. I admit it. I went from town to town looking for the big one. When it didn't show up, I moved on, yeah, often by mutual consent."

"And you never found it."

"You're supposed to ask, not tell." Harry got to his feet and towered over her. Intentionally breathing to re-establish control of the interview. He said, "But, yes. I didn't find it, it finally found me here in Pizza County. The Harlequin story found me."

From the layout room, Helen Waugaman was listening in on the conversation and trying to gauge the level of her boss's anger. A difficult thing for her to do because Harry was seated with his back to her; she couldn't see his face. She did notice that his back was rigid with stress. She didn't move from her chair, though she wondered if she ought to. But when Harry got to his feet and moved around enough for her to see his face, Helen worried he was about to have a stroke. In such a state, she worried he might do or say something he'd come to regret. If he hadn't done so already.

Chapter 15

Another Monday morning, a bright beautiful one, not a cloud in the sky. Reverend Isaiah Bartlett, broom in hand, stepped out onto the rectory porch of the First Lutheran Church of Sutersberg, that fronted toward Main Street. Reverend Bartlett, a man of diminutive size but with a big man's baritone voice and a righteous man's faith, dressed as usual in black suit and white clerical collar. He drew in a chest full of clean, clear morning air and thanked God for the gift of it, then set about his habitual Monday morning chore of sweeping the rectory stoop as penance for the sin of Sunday-sermon long-windedness.

At the same time, FBI agents Sparks and Plunkett had finished a second breakfast of coffee and donuts at the Main Street *Dunkin'Donuts*—their first, the complementary so-called Continental breakfast at the motel, was comprised of watery coffee and stale pastries. They were strolling up the street toward the Courthouse Annex. Both men were feeling full and satisfied, though the investigation that brought them to Sutersberg in the first place, the bank robberies by the person known as the Harlequin, was proceeding anything but satisfactorily.

Not that Reverend Bartlett recognized the two men, he had never seen them before, but he knew they weren't Sutersbergers. He prided himself in knowing everyone in Sutersberg, even the heathens. Neither of the two men were churchgoing Lutherans or else Reverend Bartlett would have seen them in attendance at his church the morning before. Despite their being strangers, the Reverend waved to them and called a good morning.

Ed Plunkett returned the Reverend's wave.

He said to his partner, "Y' know, Jack, I'm getting to like this place. It's…I dunno, maybe comfortable is the right word. Yeah, comfortable. Know what I mean?"

"Urp." Sparks burped and his mouth tasted of fatty donuts. Comfortable was a word that was not sitting well with him at the moment—blame Dunkin for the fatty meal, and blame the phone call he'd received at the motel the previous night from his boss at the Pittsburgh Federal Building. That call was prompted by a call his boss had received from his boss in the Hoover Building in Washington D.C.—a prime example of the old Shit-Trickles-Downhill theory. Sparks was informed by AIC Bluestone that The Washington Post had picked up a story about the Harlequin from the wire services— including a quote from *The Weekly Wise Shopper* over Harry Samuels's byline. Now everybody was laughing at the ineffectual FBI task force, not only in Harrisburg, Pennsylvania but in Washington, D.C., as well. Sparks's boss was not happy, his boss was not happy, Sparks imagined that even J. Edgar Hoover in his grave was not happy.

Sparks said, envying his partner, "You look rested this morning, Ed, much better than before. You're starting to look like a man who is gonna live. You must be sleeping better."

Plunkett shrugged. "A little, yeah, maybe. Finally. For a while there the nightmares were so bad… Every night the surgeons were cutting me open, my guts were spilling out. Every night. It got so bad I was afraid to close my eyes. You won't believe this but…"

"Oh, I believe it, all right. I had the identical problem sleeping after I was shot. Fourteen years ago. What, I never mentioned it? Yeah, I was shot shortly after my rookie year with The Bureau. In Baltimore, it was. I wasn't even on duty, I'd just gotten off. I stopped in a *7-Eleven* to buy a pack of smokes. Yeah, I smoked then, gave it up right after that. Anyhow, I walked right into a robbery in progress. A young PR kid held me and the store clerk at gunpoint while he filled his pockets from the cash register. He was jumpy from whatever he was high on, a kid of maybe nineteen, twenty?" Sparks shrugged. "A minute or two with that gun pointed at me felt like hours. I still feel it every time I think of it. That freakin' kid didn't actually mean to pull the trigger, I don't think, the gun just went off. Got me in the right side, just below and to the right of my belly button. Amputated my appendix, among other things. Remind me sometime, I'll show you my scar."

"I look forward…"

"Point is, I re-lived that shooting every night for weeks. Months." Sparks turned away from his colleague to see the incident again playing out in the sky. He murmured, "It's amazing how huge the opening at the end of a gun barrel looks when the gun is pointed at you. You notice that?"

Most of what he had said about the incident in that long ago *7-Eleven* was said lightly, as if he found it humorous, but not the last bit. That was said in deadly earnest. Sparks kept walking up Main Street, less aware of the vehicular traffic that usually occupied the attention of pedestrians. Plunkett managed to keep pace with him.

Finally Plunkett said, "You don't think our boy is really armed, do you, Jack? I don't, not really."

"Our boy, I take it you've decided to adopt him? No, I don't think he's carrying. I think if he had a gun in his pocket the way he pretends, he'd have shown it by now. For effect, y' know? Just to show he was serious."

"I agree, I guess, though I'm not so sure he's serious," Plunkett said. "I think the only kind of gun he might have is the kind, when you pull the trigger a flag drops down that says, BANG! You've seen the kind I mean on TV?"

"Yeah, I have. I only wish that PR kid in the *7-Eleven* had shot me with one of those."

Chapter 16

It was a Wednesday in the middle of that same week, a Wednesday that nearly brought disaster to the Harlequin.

His vehicle was parked in a carefully selected place, as always. Even hunkered down as he was behind the wheel, he had a clear view of the goings in and comings out of the *PNC Bank* branch in the *GeeBee* Shopping Center. The time, 1:15 p.m., was well chosen. Lunchtime was past, workers were back at work, casual diners would still be at their tables deeply in chat mode, or else they have left their tables and are on their separate ways. But either way, diners were not here, this particular shopping center had only one restaurant, a pseudo-French place with a continental menu and dinner service hours only. So, no chance of after-lunch pedestrians.

There were lots of vehicles of all types parked in the bank's lot, not only his, but none was occupied as far as he could see. So, no eyes were on the Harlequin, no one was around to see and remember the person dressed in a long-sleeved pink shirt and white painter's over-alls. On the seat beside him were items to round out this poor excuse of a costume, one he was not proud of. Not up to the now-famous Harlequin's standards: a fluff of cotton to glue to the butt of the painter's overalls, a pair of floppy cotton strips that no self-respecting rabbit would have for ears, and a sticky red glob of substance—who knew what that stuff was—for a nose. It sure didn't look like a rabbit's nose but, hell, bank tellers should be able to use a little imagination, shouldn't they?

The shopping center itself was situated off Route 30 not quite in and not quite out of Sutersberg, on its eastern edge, part of the corridor that led to Greenfield and beyond, to the Laurel Mountains.

So the time and place were well chosen, but the Harlequin felt uneasy; he felt edgy and was reluctant to move. His attention was being drawn away from crucial details. He knew that distractions could spell disaster, but he couldn't prevent his mind from wandering. Fifteen minutes had passed without his having made a single move, but so what? Was there any reason to hurry? No, and every reason for a careful surveillance.

Such was his mood, and apprehension was definitely the state he was in. Thoughts of the weather distracted him, though he couldn't blame his mood on the weather. For a western Pennsylvania August, the weather was truly typical—warm, humid and overcast; from one moment to the next either threatening or not threatening rain. Might it rain? Yes, but wait, maybe not, here comes the sun. Wearing a rainproof jacket or carrying an umbrella would label a person as a wimp, but there was no denying a heaviness to the air that felt and tasted like rain.

Such was his mood, even thoughts of the shopping center distracted him. Pizza Countians were… Sutersbergers were…

Most Pizza Countians, Sutersbergers in particular, are of one mind when it comes to the past: they are not against progress per se, but they prefer things the way they used to be. That's why the shopping center in which the Harlequin was parked was still spoken of, whenever it was spoken of, as the *GeeBee* Shopping Center. The *GeeBee* was an earlier version of a *Kmart* or a *WalMart*, a gigantic, ahead-of- its-time discount mart, locally owned and operated by the Goldberg Brothers (hence, GeeBee). The store was a thriving enterprise in the 1960s and well into the 1970s, but by the end of the 70s both brothers and the store itself were gone. They have been gone for more than sixty years, its place in the center of the mall taken by a regional chain supermarket. Still, ask most Pizza Countians or any Sutersberger where you might find the *Amish Furniture Outlet* or the *Staples Office Supply* or a branch of *PNC Bank* and they'll tell you, the *GeeBee* Shopping Cen... oh.

The Harlequin cursed himself for his lack of attention—Focus! Move! At first glance the way seemed clear. He stuck the ball of mysterious red substance on his nose, retrieved the so called—tsk—rabbit ears and cotton fluff from the passenger seat, and began to exit the car.

He had the door open and one foot on concrete when he detected movement at the corner of his right eye: someone with a rolling gait, arms swinging, walking toward the entrance to the bank. A familiar gait, a very familiar, recognizable sight. A man dressed in a brown hooded cowl, bound with a rope at the waist, his head shaved in the expected monk's tonsure, and brown sandals on his bare feet. He immediately recognized Brother Cyril, the monk who ran the Wednesday night bingo and served meals for the homeless at the First Episcopal Church. For good reason people called him Saint Cyril, to which he humbly demurred.

Observing Brother Cyril as he sashayed toward the bank—thinking, how else could one possibly walk on hard asphalt with sandals on stocking-less feet—the Harlequin became aware of other movement, this time to his left. Seeming to appear from out of nowhere (actually from just beyond four other vehicles in the Harlequin's row), that cowboy look-alike, that stooge of Chief Ianuzzi, Sergeant Poke Perkins hustled into the scene that the Harlequin was viewing through his windshield. So mindboggling to observe, like being at home with a microwave-able dinner watching *Law and*

Order on TV; watching Perkins closing in on the monk, a man in a costume about to rob a bank as far as that idiot of a cop was concerned; watching as Perkins mistook Saint Cyril for him, the Harlequin. Watching Poke twist the monk's saintly arm behind his saintly back and bring him to his saintly knees on the asphalt. Handcuffing him.

The Harlequin wished Brother Cyril well as he started his car, shifted into gear and eased quietly away. Once on Route 30 heading west toward downtown Sutersberg, the Harlequin offered up a prayer of thanks for his salvation to Saint Jude, the patron saint of all miscreants.

Chapter 17

W hat a wonderful day for a walk. It had drizzled steadily most of the previous night, but the warmth of the rising sun burned off the resultant fog, and by mid-morning, which it now was, the sky was clear, the air temperature was warm without being oppressive, and a man could be grateful and downright thrilled to be walking and breathing.

Again this morning, as Ed Plunkett strolled along Pennsylvania Avenue, his destination the office of *The Weekly Wise Shopper*, the FBI agent marveled at how comfortable a place Sutersberg was, or more to the point, how comfortable he was there. To him Sutersberg had become as comfortable as a fifteen-year-old sweatshirt. He had fallen in love with it.

When Plunkett entered the *Shopper* office, he found Harry Samuels sitting at his desk in what served as the reception area, enjoying a coffee break. Helen Waugaman was wearing the same dark brown, tent-like thing she had worn the last time he'd seen her. This time she was doing a pathetically slow dance—her dance partner a long-handled broom—first around the room, then around Harry and his desk. More than a mere dance, a ghostly waltz. Then as Plunkett watched she waltzed around her own desk, pushing dust from place to place across the worn tile floor.

Harry offered the FBI agent a cup of coffee; Plunkett spotted the jar of instant powder on Harry's desk and declined. Taking his mug with him, Harry led Plunkett out of the office and across the street toward his favorite bench in front of the library.

On the way across the avenue Plunkett said, "I don't know how you stand it." Nodding toward the office.

Harry replied, "Instant coffee does take some getting used to."

"I meant that dump you call an office."

A grin lit Harry's face. Of course he knew. He said, "Oh, that. It's like the coffee, it takes some getting used to, but you do. You can get used to anything if it's all you can afford." He swallowed a mouthful of coffee before adding, "But I have plans."

"Oh?"

"Oh, yeah. I'm not bound by a lease, so I can move to nicer quarters whenever I want to, and I'm gonna, just as soon as…well, soon."

Plunkett announced, "Ladies and gentlemen, Harry Samuels has big plans. Tada. The future looks bright, does it?"

"It just might be, yeah, if things go a certain way." Harry showed Plunkett his crossed fingers. "I intend to turn *The Shopper* into, well, I'm thinking of its future as being an opinion pamphlet. Something like a blog, only a thing of substance, in print on paper. At first a few ads and coupons will still be there, but eventually I'll transition it into a pamphlet: I'll publish opinions on politics and current events, social occasions. Trendy stuff like that."

"Well, Patrick Henry, whose opinions beside yours? I'm assuming, yours."

"Of course, mine. But other people's, the subscribers will want to exchange opinions, see their ideas in print. I'm hoping." Harry made with the crossed fingers again.

"So. When do you plan this transition from shopper to opinion pamphlet to take place? After we capture the Harlequin?" Plunkett was trying to read Harry's perpetually watery eyes for a reaction to the suggestion that the object of Harry's recent successes, the Harlequin, had no real future. "You do realize we'll eventually nab him? He can't elude our task force much longer, the odds are with us, not him."

A moment's pause, then Harry broke out in a huge grin. He said, "Did I hear on the grapevine that Sergeant Perkins slammed the cuffs on an Episcopal monk the other day? It was Brother Cyril, wasn't it?" He waited until he saw the expected frown on Plunkett's face. "The odds are with the task force, are they?" Harry lip farted. "Is anything new in the investigation, Agent Plunkett? Anything at all? An arrest, a suspect, even. Do you have any suspects, Agent Plunkett?"

Ed Plunkett's experience as an interrogator warned him not to reveal anything to Samuels, but his hackles were up and his control slipped. "Just one suspect," he barked. "You."

It worked to wipe the grin off Harry's face momentarily, then pale cheek and jowl turned to red and he found his voice. "Me? Oh, that's rich. Me?"

"You lied back in February when you said you were in the bank when the Harlequin robbed it. Implying that you both could be seen by everyone, so that you and the Harlequin couldn't possibly be one and the same person. But you weren't in the bank, were you, Harry? I think not. You were never seen at the same time as the Harlequin, and you've admitted several times to me, even in print, that you don't want us to catch him. So, yes, you are definitely a suspect."

"Did I say that I was in the bank?" Harry looked around for support, but they were alone. "I didn't, I never said that. I was outside the bank about to go in when I saw the Harlequin. He showed me a gun...all right, he didn't show it. It was in his pocket, but he aimed his pocket at me. I was not about to follow him in. You think I'm suicidal? I stayed outside and waited until I saw him leave before going in." He got quickly to his feet and faced the agent. "But, hey, I'm a suspect. That's great. I couldn't think of a subject for my editorial for this week's front page. I've got a subject now. I can see it now: Folks, your reporter is a suspect. Wait till you read it, Agent Plunkett. Just wait."

He turned and dashed across the street without looking both ways and disappeared through the door of the *Shopper* office.

Chapter 18

The end of lunchtime found Chief Dom Ianuzzi still at his desk in the Sutersberg Police Station. He had already polished off a foot-long Italian hoagie, and now he looked forward to a few minutes of quiet contemplation, his remedy to insure good digestion. He intended to follow contemplation with a little nap before returning to the pile of paperwork he'd been wading through all morning.

Ideally he would have enjoyed hunkering down in his swivel chair with both cowboy-booted feet on the desk the way he'd seen his fictional hero, Sheriff Walt Longmire as played by Robert Preston, do on TV. Unfortunately, the rotund Nuzzi had tried it once—the swivel chair, like a bucking bronco, threw him ass over tin cups backwards over onto his head. Took more than a week for the head wound to heal. So Nuzzi was forced to settle for less. He opened the lowest drawer of his desk and rested one leg on that.

Chief Ianuzzi felt the same way about Sutersberg and Piazza County as the fictional Sheriff Longmire felt about the town of Durant, Absaroka County, Wyoming—they were his town and his County. Nuzzi's life was dedicated to the town and the County; he took its law and order as his personal responsibility. With his colossal bulk, dressed as he usually was in full uniform and constantly hitching the utility rig in an effort to keep his pants up, Nuzzi could be mistaken for an object of fun. The truth was, he was a competent administrator and he ran an efficient, effective police force. He was a man of bulk, but he knew when to push that bulk around and when to pull it back; he knew when to growl and when to chuckle, when to put a hurt on someone and when to pat him on the back. Consequently, he was liked and respected in the department and in the County.

A hesitant tap before the door eased open and Tessa Waugaman peeked in. She drew a breath and was about to speak when Nuzzi interrupted her.

"Yeah, yeah, I know. You didn't mean to disturb me. Don't apologize, okay? What's it?"

Tessa loved being a member of the police force even though she was just a civilian employee. Civilian clothes would have sufficed, but she opted to wear a policewoman's uniform without unit patches and ID tags, and Nuzzi noticed how admirably well she filled out the dark blue trousers and contrasting, light blue blouse.

She said, "Sergeant Perkins is wanting to see you agin, Chief. Another apology, I expect. And a Mr. Rupert Jones wishes to see ya, on urgent business, he says. No appointment, o' course."

Nuzzi was pleased to learn that his new employee, in addition to being a looker, was also a swift learner. Tessa was a recent hire, but she was getting to know her way around the station and its personnel. However, Tessa had no way of knowing about Mr. Rupert Jones, whereas everybody else in the department knew Rupe only too well. Nuzzi asked Tessa to send Sergeant Perkins in first. He said, "And keep Mr. Jones occupied until I'm through with Perkins, okay?"

'Cowboy' was a nickname wise guys in Sutersberg might have pinned onto Sergeant Poke Perkins because of his Western look: worn leather boots, neckerchief, white Stetson hat, six-shooter holstered low on his right hip. They wisely chose not to call him 'Cowboy.'

'Weasel' was another nickname they might have stuck on Perkins, God knew the name 'weasel' certainly suited him: his every move was cautious, sneaking and, well, weasely. Again wisely, the wise guys refrained, simply because they were afraid of him. They had heard of his legendary prowess with the blackjack that he always carried on his utility belt.

Knowing that his boss was upset with him, Perkins's entrance that afternoon into Chief Ianuzzi's private sanctum was more weasely than usual.

He tiptoed into the room, saying, "Listen, Chief, I didn't..."

"No, you listen, Poke." Poke was about to take a seat, but Nuzzi stopped him. "And stay on your feet, you're not gonna be here that long.

"Chill, will ya, Poke, I'm not pissed at ya any more. I was, you bet yer ass I was, but I got over it. I realize you were just overeager, like all the rest of us. Still are, all of us, so I can't blame you for that. I'm overeager myself. You shoulda recognized Brother Cyril, you must have seen him sometimes when you're patrolling the streets. But... Brother Cyril is a most forgiving man. He doesn't want to make anything of it, so you and the department are off the hook." This got a sigh out of Perkins.

Nuzzi went on: "We're all anxious to show the Staties and the Feds that we know our stuff here in Pizza County. We all feel that way, Poke, but good judgment...."

"We own him, Chief," Poke barked, his teeth on edge as if he were biting the words. "The Harlequin belongs to us, he's our guy and we're the ones that need t'collar him, not some FBI..."

"Now, Poke, I said cool it and I mean cool it. Now, cool it!"

"Yeah, okay, Chief."

"Now, scram. You heard me, outa here. And tell Tessa to send Rupe in."

"Aw, Chief, you know what Rupe's gonna do. You know he's not…"

"Of course, he's not, Poke. I know that. But, Rupe's gotta do what Rupe's gotta do, and I got no choice but to let him do it. As usual. Tell Tessa to send him in."

Rupert Jones was a big man. Seeing him, one would suppose he had played football somewhere for someone; one supposed it, but it was a guess, no one knew for sure. He was born somewhere else and one day, seemingly from out of nowhere, he became a daily presence in Sutersberg. No one knew anything about him, and Rupe was too hulking a presence to approach with questions. Even the chief of police was not inclined to do so. Not that anyone was afraid of Rupe; not any more, not after a while. He was the gentle giant who did all the heavy lifting at the *Shop 'n Save Market* on Pittsburgh Street. He kept the parking lot clean and helped the ladies put their groceries in their cars.

Rupert was as wide as a pro lineman, though not so wide that he had to turn sidewise to fit through Nuzzi's office door, but that is the way he did enter: sidewise and stooped over. Though he was tall, he wasn't so tall that he feared bumping his head on things, but that was Rupe's way of coming and going. Old football injuries were the cause, that was what other people guessed, or maybe a brain-damaging injury, but no one knew for sure. Like other people, Nuzzi couldn't help speculating on Rupe's posture. He blamed Rupe's stoop on a massive burden of guilt he imagined Rupe was carrying.

Dom Ianuzzi had been a Sutersberg cop for twenty years. Mario Balzic was chief when he first signed on.

After five years of daily and nightly patrolling Sutersberg's streets, Nuzzi was confident he knew every living soul in town; knew when they came, when they went and if they went, when they returned. Nuzzi became aware of Rupert Jones's appearance in town ten years ago; that was when Nuzzi was acting assistant to Chief Dan Felice. In that ten year period, Rupert Jones had confessed to every major crime, and several minor acts of mayhem, lawlessness and vandalism that occurred in the County. No sooner was a crime reported in the local newspaper, on radio or TV than Rupert Jones showed up at the Police Station to make a full confession.

He entered Nuzzi's office sidewise and stooped, and greeted the police chief in the way he greeted everyone, with as few words as possible: "Nuz."

"Take a seat, Rupe. There, now tell me what's on your mind today. What can I do ya for?"

"Came to turn myself in. The banks, all them times, I did 'em. I'm yer Harlequin."

"You don't say. Well, it's damn clever of ya, Rupe, using costumes, otherwise people would've recognized you right off. A clown, the Easter bunny, yeah. But Richard Nixon, Rupe? A Republican? That was going too far. How many guys are that clever, huh? I was thinkin' about comin' for ya, Rupe."

"Well, glad I came, turned myself in."

"Go out in the hall, Rupe, and send Tessa back in here. Who's Tessa? The cute girl out there with the tight little buns, send her in, okay?"

Tessa came with Rupert in tow; she stood in the doorway keeping him in tow by a handful of the back of his shirt. Her disbelief that the gentle giant could be guilty of anything was writ large on her face.

"Escort Mr. Jones downstairs to the cells, please, Tessa. Tell whoever's working down there this afternoon... Noonan, is it? Tell Noonan to see that Rupe gets a good dinner and..."

Nuzzi could see Tessa's questions coming as she approached his desk out of Rupe's earshot. "Now, Tessa. You're right, he didn't do anything wrong. He just likes to confess. No accounting fer some people, that's a fact. I think he gets tired of his room over at the YMCA, he likes the cells. Tomorrow mornin' Poke'll drop him off in time for his shift at the *Shop 'n Save.*"

She shrugged, nodded. Nuzzi said, "Takes all kinds to make a world, Tessa. All kinds."

On her way out Tessa said, "I got a lot to learn, still, Chief. I'm tryin.' But I'd take it kindly if you'd, like, stop referring to my tight little buns. Okay?"

Nuzzi waved bye-bye to her.

Chapter 19

"**W**e have to change our tack or the ship is gonna sink."

FBI agent Jack Sparks was addressing his fellow task force members in a closed meeting—especially closed to all media reps—hastily called on Sunday evening after Sparks had received another chewing out over the phone from AIC Bluestone, his boss in Pittsburgh, who had subsequently received a chewing out from his boss in the Hoover Building in Washington, D.C. Blank stares told Sparks that the nautical terms he used were not well chosen. Sutersberg was a landlocked town and there were few sailors in Pizza County. Truth be told, he didn't know where the nautical terms came from or why he used them, not being a sailor himself.

"First, lemme tell you, I've had it up to here with the bitching at me for calling this meeting on Sunday night. Let's agree to restrain all bitching till we've caught the Harlequin, okay? And believe me, we've gotta catch him pronto. My boss back in the 'burgh just informed me, the paperwork for my transfer to the Island of Guam is on his desk ready for his signature. So, yeah, we either change our tack or our ship sinks. Am I clear, do we all get it now?" They did. All of a sudden his meaning was clear.

"We've been operating the way experienced cops are supposed to operate in pursuit of a perp: we made assumptions as to the Harlequin's intentions and we did our best to counter those intentions. When that failed, we assumed we just needed to keep at it, the odds favored us. So we thought. But there are so many damn bank branches all over our three counties, and we're so under-staffed, no way could we possibly cover them all. That's what we figured. We never thought our failure was due to misunderstanding our perp's intentions, but now I'm convinced we did, I think we got our perp's intentions completely wrong."

This caused the crowd to stir, some nods, some men, at a complete loss, gaped. A low buzz could be heard in the room.

"I should give credit where it's due here: my FBI colleague, Ed Plunkett, was the man who caught on to this mother... uh, this guy's intentions almost from the start. He kept telling me, 'It's not the money, it's not the money.' He was telling me that, but I wasn't listening." A lot of heads turned toward Plunkett, who as usual was seated in a folding chair at the back of the room. "Well, I'm listening now, Ed. We're gonna start a new way of thinking about the Harlequin and a new way of pursuing him.

"First step, let's look at what we know about the Harlequin, or at least what we think we know."

One of the civilian employees rolled a white board over to the center of the conference room from its out-of-the-way place in a corner. She handed Sparks a black grease marker. Everyone in the room could now see as Sparks wrote on it:

Motivation

He said, "From now on we are going to operate on the assumption that money is not what motivates the Harlequin. Yeah, like everybody else in this world, he prob'ly needs it; maybe he needs it more than most of us. But we don't think he's motivated by that need. Why? Because he hasn't been choosing which banks to target by when or where the most money could be had, nor has he been hitting the banks at a time when the most money was available. In fact he's been doing just the opposite, hitting the little out-of-the- way branches early in the day before they've done much business. What's really motivating him, we think—we hope—is maybe the publicity or the kicks he's gotten from the notoriety. This may make him a nut case, but he's a smart nut case.

"Second," Sparks wrote again on the board:

We Think We Know Him

"We wonder, Why doesn't he just wear a mask? Why all the trouble to assemble a costume? Okay, he's a nut, but still. It's a lot of trouble to go to, so we think maybe there's another reason. Maybe we know the guy well enough, maybe everybody in the County knows him well enough so that if he just wore a mask, we'd still recognize him. But if he covers up most of his entire body...get it? Like if...uh, say Chief Ianuzzi, here, was the Harlequin. If he just wore a mask we'd still recognize him, but if he completely covered up..."

Someone shouted, "We'd still recognize him, or think we were dealing with Orca the Whale." Everyone laughed, even Nuzzi did, but only after spinning around in his seat to get a bead on the shouter.

Sparks continued, "That's how we're thinking at this point when we say the Harlequin may be a prominent citizen, maybe even an elected official."

He stepped to the white board again, wrote on it:

We Think He Knows Us

He underlined the word us and said, "For the same reason, because we think he's a prominent citizen, we think he knows us. By that we don't mean an in-general us, we mean specifically us, we mean the task force members. He not only has a good idea of how law enforcement officers think and work, we think he knows a lot of us personally, you and me, us, the members of the task force. He knows us, he knows our vehicles, he knows our faces. When he first shows up at the scene of a robbery, he doesn't first scope out the bank, he scopes out the vicinity looking for us."

Sparks put down the marker and stepped away from the board. Slapping his hands as if they were coated with chalk powder, he said, "That pretty much sums up our thinking at this point, and it's the way we want the task force to operate from now on:

First, don't use the amount of money a bank is holding at any given time to select which bank branches to stake out. The little isolated places are more likely the targets of the Harlequin.

Second, be careful to conceal yourselves when you're on stakeout. Stay as much out of sight as possible, maybe even wear civilian clothes.

Third, don't use official vehicles, use your personal vehicles; better yet, borrow your mother-in-law's vehicle.

"That's all I've got, we're done here, fellas and gals. Keep those points in mind when you go on patrol, and maybe we'll finally catch this sonofabitch.

"Oh, and once again putting credit where it's due: Total credit for our change of thinking about the Harlequin goes to my FBI colleague, Ed Plunkett. Three cheers for him. Hip Hip."

And total blame on Ed Plunkett if our changed thinking doesn't work, Ed thought. They cheered him, all right, but Plunkett knew they were thinking as he did. His ass was on the line.

Chapter 20

She didn't have to beg. FBI agent Sparks was not willing or not able, due to time constraints, to grant E.G. McManus—a.k.a. EmmaGrace—an interview, but he gladly suggested Agent Plunkett to take his place. Plunkett seemed willing enough. He agreed to meet her mid-morning at the *Starbucks* across Route 30 from the motel where the agents were billeted.

Plunkett arrived a few minutes past the appointed ten o'clock hour; after getting a grande regular coffee with cream and artificial sweetener, he approached the booth the student reporter was occupying and slid in across from her.

The orange Afro-ed Orphan Annie look-alike was wearing a green sweatshirt with Grove City on the chest in white block letters. She said, "How do you know you're at the right table?"

"Listen, girlie. You happen to be speaking to a federal agent with years of investigative experience." Plunkett exaggerated a look-around for eavesdroppers. "Besides, you're the only customer in the place." She blushed, kicking herself for walking into that one. She had so wanted to impress him with her professionalism.

Plunkett said, "I agreed to the interview but I wasn't told what media you represent." When she didn't reply he prompted: "Well what, a newspaper? TV station? What?"

"I sorta represent Grove City University? Or maybe its Department of Journalism? Take your pick.

Hopefully this interview will end up, maybe, I hope, in *The Grove City Collegian*?" She shrugged.

"*The Collegian*? Grove City? You mean little Grove City, up north toward Erie? What are you doing here, little girl?" With his stern-father's tone, Plunkett meant to force her into a submissive position. Instead, it forced EmmaGrace to dig in her heels. She tried to show a stiff upper lip. After all, she wasn't really EmmaGrace, she was E.G. McManus.

She said, "I'm not your little girl, I'm not anybody's little girl, I'll have you know. I'm a grad student and my professor sent me down here. I'm supposed to get some practical experience by working with Harry Samuels. They, Professor Terwelliger and Mr. Samuels, they used to work together. Once or twice, a while back."

"Hey, apologies." Plunkett backed off. "No offense meant. But, you're working for Samuels? For the *Shopper*?"

"Not for Mr. Samuels, with Mr. Samuels. I'm sorta covering your task force and the pursuit of the Harlequin. Mr. Samuels looks over my work, gives me pointers? That kinda thing."

"I see." Plunkett nodded, thinking he knew who he was speaking with, now. "Well, okay, first some ground rules." She nodded. "You understand the meaning of on the record and off the record?" He insisted on waiting for a nod before proceeding. "Then I'll expect you to honor that. Also, Do you understand the difference between my being deliberately evasive, on the one hand, and my need to withhold information from the general public, on the other?"

After a pause she said, "Help me out with that one."

He was glad to. A corner of his mouth turned up in the struggle not to chuckle. "There's a fine line of difference. For instance, you ask a question the answer to which will make me look bad or incompetent, so I don't answer. That's evasion. On the other hand, you ask a question that I really want to answer, but if I did the general public would know, the Harlequin would know, so I don't answer. That's a necessary withholding of information from the general public."

Consternation spread across E.G.'s waif-like face. "But either way the result is, like, the same: like, you don't answer the question."

"True enough. As I said, it's a fine line of difference. That fine line is the territory that experienced reporters operate in. It's probably why that professor of yours from Grove City sent you down here to work with Harry Samuels: so you can learn to work between the lines, so to speak. You think?"

"I don't...get it, no. Lookit, Mister big shot FBI man." Her color was up now. "I know when I'm being put on. I wasn't born yesterday."

If not yesterday, the day before, Plunkett thought. He decided to let that pass and told her to go ahead and ask her questions.

"You mean you actually intend to answer them? No more put ons?"

"Try me."

"Alright. After months of investigation, do you have any idea who the Harlequin is? Any idea at all?"

"No, we don't, but that's not important, or not as important as you think it is. We know we won't identify him from clues he leaves behind. He doesn't leave clues behind. He hasn't so far and probably won't. We have to catch him in the act. So, you see, his identity is only secondary as far as the investigation is concerned. Is that clear?"

Doubt cut a deep line between E.G.'s eyes. "You expect to catch him in the act, do you? Optimistic, aren't you. Has something happened to make you so optimistic? Something new?"

"Not something new, exactly, not an actual thing like a happening. Hmm, put it this way: A new way of thinking about the Harlequin leads me to be confident that his arrest is imminent."

"Imminent? That sounds, like, inevitable, wouldn't you say? You're certain. Well, if it's inevitable and imminent, surely the Harlequin is smart enough to know that. Why doesn't he just quit?"

"He would if he could, but he can't."

Her eyes bore into him. "I get it. You think he's crazy, don't you?"

Plunkett took a swallow of coffee, now grown cold, and nodded. "Not stark raving mad, but, yeah, I think he's more than a little bit crazy. That is off the record, understand? No sense pissing him off by saying I think he's nuts in print."

"But that's the only interesting thing you've said so far, and it's off the record? Thanks a lot. Can I at least say, the FBI thinks the Harlequin's arrest is imminent and he should do the right thing by turning himself in?"

"You can say that on the record. Between you and me, though, and that means this is off the record…" An exaggerated glance over his shoulder for eaves-droppers. "… the wisest thing the Harlequin could do right now would be to simply stop robbing banks.

"Just stop, for Chrissake, and disappear for good and forever. With the little we know about you and who you are, we'll never catch you. The Harlequin will become a thing of Pizza County legend. A mystery never to be solved."

Plunkett stared at her. "That's definitely off the record," he said and winked at her. "Little girl, you don't want to repeat that to anyone."

Chapter 21

Immediately after the FBI man, Plunkett, had agreed to an interview, EmmaGrace scheduled a sit down with Harry Samuels for the following day. Professor Terwelliger had suggested she do so—suggested it with a capital S and an exclamation point! EmmaGrace wasn't happy about it. Who wanted or needed some worn out, old, had-been, once-was looking over her shoulder? She could just imagine the damp feel of Harry's old breath on the nape of her neck—she shivered at the thought. But...what heads of departments want, heads of departments get.

Harry Samuels hadn't been too keen on the idea of his editing her work, either. Harry remembered that ScottTerwelliger had an edgy sense of humor that had always put Harry off. He wondered: maybe Terwelliger had referred the hard-to-be-taken-serious waif, the Orphan Annie look-alike, to Harry, aware of his present low station in the profession, hoping that seeing how far he had fallen would turn EmmaGrace off journalism— or would rid journalism of her—for good and forever. How cruel, if Terwelliger meant to use Harry that way. How cruel to both of them, really, but he wouldn't put it past the Scott Terwelliger he remembered.

So, precisely at 11:00 a.m. of the morning following the interview, two reluctant people, EmmaGrace (a.k.a. E.G.) McManus and Harry Samuels, after a bit of furniture re-arranging, sat down beside one another at his battered wooden desk in the office of *The Weekly Wise Shopper*. She told him everything that had been said in the interview, both on the record and off.

They did not pore over a draft of her article, there was no article to pore over, just a few lonely-looking, scribbled lines on one page in her three-by-five-inch notebook. Nothing much to work with, but it suddenly changed everything: EmmaGrace was no longer reluctant—she knew she needed help and the only source for that help was Harry Samuels.

Harry, too, was no longer reluctant. He was experiencing, possibly for the first time in his life, an affirmation that his knowledge and the experience of his lifetime struggles in journalism were gifts of real value and, too, there was real satisfaction to be had in passing those gifts along to an eager student.

"There isn't much here, E.G.," Harry said after a cursory glance at her notes. "But...not to worry. In our business we never have enough facts for the amount of space we're allotted. It's a fact of life in journalism. It's either not enough fresh facts and too much space, or too many facts and not enough space, or..." He tossed an arm to dismiss that line of thought.

"Any idea how much space the editor of *The Grove City Collegian* intends to allow for your story?"

"No idea how much, no idea if he has any intention for it," she said glumly.

"Don't be discouraged, that only necessitates that we keep it brief, which is just as well. No editor will ever curse you for brevity, that I guarantee. So.

"Jot this down in your little notebook, so you'll have it to refer to whenever you're composing, now and in future. Okay?

"First: Begin with a paragraph re-hashing the case beginning with the first holdup after Christmas last year. About one hundred words, tops. Always begin your pieces with a short re-hash paragraph to get the attention of readers that aren't familiar with your subject. There will always be people that aren't, like now. Lots of Grove City people aren't familiar with the Harlequin. They're up north, not in Pizza County. Right?" E.G. conceded the point with a shrug.

"Follow that paragraph with one that contains the most fascinating of your new facts, if there are any new facts. If there's nothing new, you have to find a way to make the old facts fascinating. For our present situation, maybe comment on how protracted the pursuit of the Harlequin has been, how it has dragged on and on and... you get the idea, and how about the new approach to the pursuit, the new way of thinking that Plunkett mentioned? He did say that was on the record, didn't he? Well then, use it. But use it to your advantage, not his."

EmmaGrace didn't get what he meant by her advantage.

Harry said, "Well, for instance, like this: 'Considering how long the pursuit of...no, the fruitless pursuit of the Harlequin has dragged on, and the fact that no specific details were given by the government agent to support the supposed new approach of the task force, one can only wonder if...'" Like that. Use Plunkett's on-the-record statement as a way into a little doubtful speculation on your part. Write it that way and believe me, if the editor of *The Grove City Collegian* is worth his salt as a newspaper man, you'll see an E.G. McManus byline on his front page, above the fold."

She replied, "Well...." The face she turned to Harry looked even more lost than usual. "That's all well and good, but I'm missing something here. I've got a feeling, like, I just arrived at the station but the train's gone and left me behind. What am I missing?"

Harry knew what she was missing, of course he did. She was asking what she was missing, but he wondered if she actually knew. And if she knew, did she think he knew? And if she did know that he knew, he wondered if he ought to tell her what he knew. And if she didn't know but knew that he knew, he wondered what he ought to tell her, and if he ought to tell her what, he wondered if he ought to...

Harry had to derail that train of thought because his brain was threatening to jump its track.

He said, "Have you given any thought to why Agent Plunkett granted you that interview in the first place? If there was nothing new to report and he had little if anything to say, at least nothing much on the record, why grant the interview? To a student, yet? C'mon. Tell me again what he said, this time just the stuff that he said was off the record."

Dawn was breaking in EmmaGrace's eyes. Harry thought she was beginning to catch on. He said, "Yeah, give that some thought, the answers are significant. At least in my opinion they are."

She started to retell what Plunkett had said about the Harlequin's mental condition, but that wasn't the part he considered significant. She said, "You mean the part about the Harlequin stopping holding up banks, just stopping and disappearing, and the authorities would never be able to identify him? That's, like, the significant part?"

"Yep, I think that's it. You don't get it, do you? That was for me. He knew you'd tell me what he said, he wanted you to. He couldn't rightly tell that to me himself, it would be aiding and abetting the enemy. But he could tell you, knowing you would tell me."

"But, like, why would he want to tell you that? He..."

"If you'd done your homework like any good reporter would before going into that interview, like for instance, if you'd've read the editorials I published on the front pages of *The Shopper*... If you had studied up on who, the actual person, you were going to talk to before you talked to Agent Plunkett, maybe then you'd have realized what he was doing and why:

"He was showing me a way out, E.G. He was passing a message to me through you. A warning and a way out, don't you see? You're dense as a door. He thinks I'm the Harlequin."

"But..."

"He thinks I'm the Harlequin. Jeez, EmmaGrace, you are, you're dense as a door. He thinks I'm the Harlequin."

She gaped at him. "B-but..." she sputtered, "you're not...are you?"

"Whether I am or not, who gives a damn, do you? But, oh, wouldn't that be a scoop for E.G. McManus of *The Grove City Collegian*!?"

Chapter 22

It was four o'clock of a Friday afternoon, and for most of the townsfolk it was the end of the workday at the end of the workweek. After searching the entire Courthouse Annex in hope of locating District Attorney Grimes and failing to find him, EmmaGrace McManus sighed in frustration and muttered to herself, TGIF.

The sun hanging listlessly over Sutersberg seemed to agree, TGIF. To see it hanging in the sky off to the west, EmmaGrace thought the sun looked hard pressed to prevent its own premature sinking. While the sun still had the weekend to get through, the people who worked in the Courthouse and the people employed in the municipal offices in the Annex had no such concerns. TGIF. That dog license you were looking to purchase, that marriage license or building permit you were after, they'll have to wait until the start of another week. So, too, will your search for an attorney to press your case, for a jury to hear it or a judge to adjudicate. The clerks, the attorneys, the judges, to a man or woman, have all gone to *Mr.Frog's Pub* around the corner on Otterman Street.

On her way there, EmmaGrace paused at the intersection of Main and Otterman Streets for the light to change. Taking a deep breath, she tested the air and swore she could taste a hint of rotting leaves on the tip of her tongue. The summer was nearing its end and the leaves of deciduous trees had begun to wither and die. Kids would soon be back in their classrooms, corn and pumpkins would soon be coming to harvest. She couldn't help wondering if the Harlequin would soon be coming to harvest, too.

Such a large, noisy crowd in *Mister Frog's*, a standing-room-only crowd, and already at four o'clock a more than a little tipsy crowd. It looked as if the entire Pizza County legal system were jammed into *Mr. Frog's* modest-sized barroom. EmmaGrace McManus, small as she was, found it difficult to squeeze inside.

District Attorney John Grimes was a head taller than most of the revelers in the crowd that surrounded him. He was loathe to tear himself away, but he had agreed to an interview, so he was watching for EmmaGrace. He spotted her as soon as she squeezed past the front door. Even in a crowded pub at Happy Hour on a Friday afternoon, an Orphan Annie look-alike with a full head of orange hair was not hard to spot.

He pushed his way through the crowd toward where her inward progress had been stymied. As soon as he drew near, EmmaGrace started scolding him. He couldn't understand a word she said over the noisy crowd, but he could see she was upset. Grimes pushed the door open and led her out to the sidewalk.

Rush hour was in full force and the fifteen-foot-wide sidewalk in front of *Mr. Frog's* felt like a third lane of traffic. Grimes apologized for not being more specific about where they were to meet. Even accounting for the slightly round-shouldered Lincoln-esque posture Grimes displayed in public, he was so much taller than EmmaGrace, he roofed over her as he spoke. He said, "I assumed everybody knew: Friday afternoons in Pizza County, all business is conducted at *Mr. Frog's*."

She took in the Grimes persona—the blue three-piece pinstripe suit, his signature white socks peeking out beneath the trouser cuffs, his lean farmer's frame, the course, homely face and appealing brown eyes. She took in the whole Grimes persona and like most of his Pizza

County constituents, she was awed to be within arm's reach of Honest Abe.

"You have questions for me?" Grimes spoke as if he couldn't imagine anyone having questions for innocent old him. "Well, ask away."

"Like, er, As a member of the Harlequin task force..."

"Whoa up there, young lady. Marge Bash represents the District Attorney's Office on the task force. My role is strictly ex-officio until they capture him. Until then..."

"You actually think they will capture him? Seems to me the pursuit of the Harlequin, up to now at least, has been rather half-hearted."

"I don't deny that, but keep in mind, the pursuit of Robin Hood was half-hearted, the pursuit of Zorro was half-hearted. They were local heroes, robbing the rich and giving to the poor. To my knowledge the Harlequin hasn't given anything to the poor, but he's become something of a local hero. But sooner or later they all get caught, believe you me."

An eighteen-wheeler came puffing and farting up the street past *Mr. Frog's*, D.A. Grimes tried not to breathe until it had passed.

"Once they get him, then and only then, it'll be a tussle between me and the U.S. Attorney in Pittsburgh as to which jurisdiction prosecutes him."

Not being a lawyer, EmmaGrace wasn't aware of this and it showed on her face.

Grimes said, "Y'see, most of the robberies were committed in my jurisdiction, Piazza County; not all, but most, so I have a long oar in the boat, so to speak. But bank robbery is a federal offense, so the U.S. Attorney has an oar in, too. We'll fight it out for the privilege..."

"What privilege? There's a considerable expense involved in prosecuting a case, any case, isn't there? If so, what's the privilege, and why would you want it?"

"Well... there's the publicity, of course. Nothing wrong with a little o' that, hmm? But no, I'd want the privilege so's I could go easy on the Harlequin, charge him with fewer and lesser crimes, whenever possible, like that. That would be what the voters of Pizza County would want me to do.

"Don't look so shocked. This is my County, I was born and raised here; I know my people. Believe me, Pizza Countians will want me to go easy on their local hero, and that's what I hope to do. The U.S. Attorney ain't from around here, who knows what kinda high horse he's riding.

"I'm ready and willing to tussle with the Federal Gov'ment for the privilege of going easy on the Harlequin," Grimes declared, "and that little item, young lady, is off the record."

Chapter 23

The Harlequin hated shopping online. Those idiots at *L.L.*Bean and *Amazon* and *Zappos* always send the wrong model in the wrong color, or the damn thing just doesn't fit. He preferred to shop at the Piazza County Mall, though neither he nor anyone else local ever called it that. He and they all knew it as the Pizza Mall. Given his preference for shopping at the mall and the fact that, as far as he knew, the layout of its *VitaBank* branch was unique in all of western Pennsylvania, he had decided to rob it. He was determined to.

What was unique about *VitaBank's* mall layout? The bank fronted into the mall's main corridor so that customers could enter from inside the mall, but they could also do their banking from the back parking lot at the rear of the mall, where there was both a walk-in entry and a drive-thru.

His intention was to rob that bank in such a way that put his exploits in the *Guinness Book of World Records*— he intended to rob it by the drive-thru. No one, not even Bonnie Parker and Clyde Barrow, had ever tried a drive-thru stickup. Already he could feel the warmth of his imminent world fame enwrapping him; he could see its aura oozing from him, flooding the passenger compartment of his *Alamo* rental.

Yes, he was driving an *Alamo* sedan that he rented for this special occasion, thinking it would look poorly if it were reported that he had pulled off the robbery of a bank by the drive-thru in an eight-year-old car. Too bad he couldn't have approached the *Alamo* folks to sponsor the caper; they'd love a mention along with the Harlequin in *The Guinness Book*. Might even want to reward him with a free weekend rental, something like that.

The Harlequin surveilled the rear of the *VitaBank* through the windshield of his *Alamo* sedan from the spot he had chosen in the rear parking lot. Stared in particular at the drive-thru window and the pretty young brunette sitting in that window.

She looked familiar. Did he know her? Yeah, it was John Barclay from the *Agway*, his daughter, Peggy. Coincidence? Not really. Typical of Pizza County, where everybody knows everybody. Peggy Barclay was chatting animatedly with each customer, receiving pneumatic canisters from the long, clear plastic umbilical; she was busily loading and unloading the canisters, firing them back, chatting some more, receiving other canisters from the umbilical, firing them back. Again and again.

The Harlequin started his sedan and began cruising at parade speed up and down the aisles of parked vehicles, waving at nonexistent adoring crowds as he'd seen Queen Elizabeth the Second doing on TV. He was barely managing to attend to job one, which was searching the cars as he drifted past for members of law enforcement, possibly the familiar faces of Harlequin task force members dressed in civilian clothes and occupying civilian vehicles. As far as he could see, once again not one task force member was in the right place at the right time.

He coasted into the drive-thru lane. He was third in line. He was grateful for a little time to try on the fit of the mask he'd bought at the *Party Store* on Route 30. Shit! Who was the idiot who thought one size fit all? One size didn't fit all at all, here was proof. The mask was too wide, it sagged on his face...or was it just that his face was too narrow? On the one hand...

He was now number two in line.

...On the other hand, the loose folds of rubber made Sean Penn look older and chinless.

Peggy Barclay, the pretty young teller, received a pneumatic canister, removed something from it, tapped a code into her keypad, fired the canister back through the plastic umbilical.

He was next in line and suddenly in a panic.

What was he doing? This was crazy, unsafe, unsafe, crazy! Emergency! Emergency!

Improvising, he dug a twenty-dollar bill from his pants pocket, stuffed it into the canister and fired it to Peggy. She plucked the twenty from the canister without looking his way.

She said, "Did you forget to include a deposit slip? You did...." She finally looked over to see who it was. She would recognize Sean Penn anywhere; this was not him, this—she recognized immediately—was the Harlequin. Not surprised and not panicked, she said, "Oh, it's you. I don't suppose you wanna, like, deposit this?"

He replied, almost using her name, "Pe..uh, no, no, I just need smaller bills, if you don't mind."

"No trouble. Do you want twenty ones? Or four fives or, like, two fives and a ten?"

The Harlequin started giggling, couldn't stop. He said, "Since it's no trouble, like, heh-heh, I'll take two tens and a five. Heh-heh."

Chapter 24

"I dunno," Ed Plunkett said, the FBI agent obviously troubled by…something. He shook his head in a vain attempt to clear his brain, as if shaking a snow globe would clear away the snow. He said to his partner across their two-fer lunch table, "Maybe it's a sign of creeping senility, or maybe it's an indication of how complicated the world has become—too damn complicated for this mother's son."

His partner's mouth was full; Sparks merely shrugged.

Plunkett went on, "Better yet, maybe the nine-mm slug that young punk fired into my belly last year was an omen. I should've taken early retirement."

Jack Sparks had no idea what was bugging his partner. The two FBI men had spent the morning, wasted it actually, at the Piazza County Mall interviewing Miss Peggy Barclay, the pretty young teller who had faced the Harlequin, albeit through bulletproof glass at a distance of fifteen feet. They learned nothing from her; they knew no more after terminating the interview than they did before.

Now they were at lunch near the mall in one of the *Primanti Bros.* restaurants, famous throughout western Pennsylvania for their humongous-sized sandwiches crowned with French fries. The noise from the bar, the noise of conversations from the tables that surrounded their own, as well as Plunkett's mumblings, all were making it tough for Agent Sparks to savor his lunch. He didn't appreciate that.

Was Plunkett crapping about the food? Sparks wasn't sure. He said, "So what if the fries are soggy, they have t' be; can't be helped. Crisp fries would slide right out of the sandwich. No reason to…"

Plunkett waved that off. "I find myself thinking, 'Faced with a decision, any decision, to do one thing or the other, any more I'm likely to make the wrong one. No confidence in my own judgment, no confidence in myself anymore. I might's well flip a coin as use my brain to make decisions. Make it easier on myself that way. Y'know what I mean? I should've spoken to this person, instead I spoke to that person. Now look how that turned out, lookit the shit I stepped in this time. That slug in the gut was an omen, I tell ya. I should've put in for early retirement."

In his long career in the FBI Sparks had had his share of moody partners, so he was not about to take Plunkett's mood too seriously. Not at first, anyway.

He said, "Oh, yeah, I agree. Being shot in the stomach at close range is an omen, all right. A very bad omen. But early retirement… Why not tell me what's eating you, Ed, and talk about early retirement later. What say?"

Plunkett tugged a French fry out from beneath his bun, dipped its soggy end in ketchup, but decided against eating it; he let it splat onto his plate.

He said, "I did something I'm not supposed to do, but I did it and I'm glad I did." Sparks didn't react to that. "The thing I did didn't work, so now I think I did the right thing the wrong way, if you get my drift." No, Sparks didn't. He shrugged, so Plunkett said, "If I tell you what I did, you won't like it." Still Sparks said nothing, just waited.

"Okay. You know for a couple months now I've been sure I know who the Harlequin is…"

"Yeah, you think it's Harry Samuels. You persist in calling him the Harlequin without even a shred of evidence, nothing."

"Right, I persist without a shred of evidence and despite the fact that I like the guy personally, and I mean that sincerely, I really do like Samuels. Not only did I come up with Harry Samuels as the Harlequin but, if you recall, I'm the one came up with the idea that he was robbing banks not for money but for the notoriety, the attention he was getting in the media."

Sparks nodded enthusiastically, willing to give credit where he thought it was due. Not only willing, but hoping to. "I hadn't forgotten that it was your idea; changed the whole direction of the taskforce, that did. Your idea."

"But what if I was wrong about that, at least at the outset. What if he was actually desperate for money? What if the robberies themselves weren't netting him very much money, but the publicity was paying off. People were paying attention to him, people were suddenly reading *The Weekly Wise Shopper*, advertisers were buying ads. For once he was getting attention and making money. What if that?"

"Well..."

Excited now, Plunkett went on, "Suddenly *The Shopper* was a profitable enterprise, and most important as far as Harry was concerned, he was suddenly a journalist again, not a sleazy advertising salesman but a journalist. The international wire services had seen the humor and, yeah, the irony in the Harlequin's antics. He was quoted in news articles in a bunch of big city papers. Harry Samuels was a journalist again. Maybe I'm pushing it hard, but it seems to me that disappointment can make a man crazy, make him do things he wouldn't ordinarily do... crazy things."

Sparks handed Plunkett his water glass and insisted he take a swallow. He said, "Ed, you're sounding like his defense attorney. You're making a good case for a mental incompetence plea. That's not your job."

After the mouthful of water Plunkett took a deep breath. "I think I might've lost sight of that fact."

"You think you might've?" Sparks didn't know what was coming, but he doubted it would be good news for the Harlequin investigation, for the taskforce or for certain FBI agents' careers. Without realizing he had done so, he clenched his right hand into a fist—maybe to pound the table, maybe to pound his partner, he wasn't sure which. In a voice heavy with apprehension, he said, "Well, let's have it, what'd ya do?"

"I sent him a message."

It was a role reversal to say the least for Ed Plunkett, confessing rather than interrogating, but it felt as if he had unloaded a lifetime of sins to confess his entire scheme to Jack Sparks: that he had used the interview with the Orphan Annie look-alike, EmmaGrace McManus, to send the message to Harry Samuels that law enforcement had absolutely no evidence as to the identity of the Harlequin; that if he simply stopped his shenanigans, stopped robbing banks, and if he disappeared into thin air he would never be identified. He'd be in the clear and untouchable.

Plunkett said, "I figured he'd be more likely to believe it and take the advice if it didn't come directly from me, but came, like, tangentially."

"Tangentially, yeah, I see." While it was true enough, they had nothing concrete to take to a judge in hope of getting even a search warrant let alone an arrest warrant, still, sending messages to suspects, even to people who were only possible suspects, was a no-no. His partner had stepped way out of bounds. He supposed not only Ed, himself, but the Federal Bureau of Investigation better take that slug to Plunkett's stomach as an omen. They'd better retire him.

But Plunkett wasn't done. He said, "I even told her, whatsername, McManus. I told her what I said was off the record, that way I figured she'd do just the opposite and repeat everything I said to Samuels, word for word." He waited while Sparks took a pull on his beer. Then said, "But maybe my advice came too late, maybe this latest thing at *VitaBank's* drive-thru is the proof in the pudding: Samuels is too far gone mentally to take anybody's advice. Like I said before: disappointment can make a man crazy."

Sparks heaved a sigh of relief, hearing that Plunkett hadn't actually sent a message to the suspect himself. He nodded, though now he wasn't convinced of the veracity of anything his partner said.

"That's one theory, he's too crazy to take anybody's advice. Or maybe she, that McManus girl, maybe she honored your off-the-record request. Maybe she didn't pass along your message. That ever occur to you, Ed?"

It hadn't.

Sparks went on, "Or maybe she did tell him, but he's not crazy. And while we're doing maybes, how about this one: maybe Harry Samuels isn't the Harlequin. Has that one ever occurred to you, Ed? Had you thought of that possibility?"

It was plain on Plunkett's face—No, he hadn't thought of that one, either.

Chapter 25

Jeez, what a night! There are so many stars, and not a cloud in sight.

It's awfully quiet in town. Always is this time of night. Vehicle traffic is at a trickle, especially at this end of town. Eighteen-wheelers that chuff and wheeze in and out of town all day are content to take the nights off. Shops are closed, folks have had their dinners and are settled down in front of the TV. Kids have been called in from their street games; they are snacked, bathed and bedded. They are sleepers tonight, scholars tomorrow. It's almost September. They will straggle up both sides of Main Street to the top of the hill, Bishop Piazza Catholic kids on one side of Main, Sutersberg Public School kids on the other.

It's awfully dark and quiet tonight, especially at this far end of Pennsylvania Avenue. Even darker than usual due to teenage vandalism. Some kid had tied an old rotten pair of sneakers into a bola and had flung it up to dangle limply from the telephone wires. That same vandal, darn fool, or one of his cohorts, had used a b-b gun or slingshot or such a weapon to blast out the nearest streetlamp. From the bench in front of the Public Library, Harry Samuels's favorite spot, one of Police Chief Ianuzzi's uniformed minions can be seen moving silently, purposefully in the shadows on foot patrol, peering in storefront windows, rattling doors, testing locks.

The moon is a sliver in the sky, waxing or waning—who remembers which is which? Helen Waugaman ends her slapdash wipe down of the *The Shopper* office and snaps off its lights. She locks the door and ambles out of sight toward her home. As for the rest of the block, there are no readers at the Public Library this time of night, none at the Christian Science Reading Room, either, and no prospects for the Army Recruiting Center.

Harry is sharing the bench with his young colleague, E.G. McManus. She is dressed in her usual retro style, looking as if she were torn from the comics page of an old newspaper that has been left out too long in the wind. Harry's tan windbreaker jacket is draped over her shoulders against the chill of the night. Sitting on the bench as she is, erect with her back against the back of the bench, her tiny feet are dangling, barely scraping the ground; on them is a pair of orange canvas Keds that closely match her orange afro. On the ground beside the bench is her battered travel case. Her intention is to catch the *Erie & Lackawanna* Late Nite Special that passes through town on its way north, back to Grove City College. In a half hour or so Harry will, or so he promised, drive her to the train station.

Her assignment for Professor Terwelliger and *The Grove City Collegian* is completed—diligently and professionally, she thinks, and Harry agrees, especially since most of what Agent Plunkett had told her was off the record, not to be quoted in print.

But Harry has other plans for her.

Startled by him, she says in a harsh whisper, "You're offering me a job? On *The Shopper*?"

"Who said anything about *The Shopper*? No, *The Shopper* is going to morph into..." Harry stands and makes like a magician pulling a rabbit out of a hat by its ears. "...Voila! *The Piazza County Crier!*" He sits back down. "How do you like the name, The *Crier*? Catchy but not too catchy, right? I thought first to go with the more familiar, The Town *Crier*, but that felt too limiting.

I wanted the new weekly paper to encompass the entire County, from Herminie to Mount Pleasant to Lower Burrell to..." Expansive arm gestures. Just talking about it makes Harry feel limitless, expansive. "...To the whole of Pizza County. I expect to have *The Crier* up and running before Thanksgiving."

She says, "I suppose you've got the financing all lined up? That's miraculous, Harry." She sounds dubious. "I thought you were all maxed out."

Harry shakes his head in denial, or EmmaGrace thinks he does. It is hard to tell for sure in the dark. He says, "My credit cards were maxed out, not me. Learn to be precise, E.G. It's a dying virtue but a real asset in our business. As for me, I've still got some spark left. I'll have you know I've managed to get all *The Shopper's* bills paid. It's free and clear."

"I wonder how you managed to do that." It is said under her breath and really wasn't a question. She thinks she knows the answer, but she didn't intend to force a confession from him. She hopes he hasn't heard her.

He hasn't or pretends not to have, and directs his attention to the sky, where it is obvious his dreams of *The County Crier's* future prospects have soared.

He says, "I want it so bad I can taste it. I feel as if I could reach up and pluck the first issue out of the air." He looks in her direction over the top of his glasses as if to see her reaction in spite of the dark. "I can just see it: a banner headline over the lead story, front page above the fold..." He peers at EmmaGrace. "...by E.G. McManus."

Something like this:

Just like the Piazza County Harlequin, the *Weekly Wise Shopper* rides off into the sunset.

This startles her. "My byline? Why me?"

Harry ignores her. "Or maybe you'd prefer to strike a more humorous tone:"

This reporter wonders: Is the Harlequin retired and living at Saint Anne's? Ha-ha.

"Why offer me a job? Why me?"

Harry takes a calming breath.

He says, "Why not you? You learn fast, you're smart, you're not lazy, you do your homework. And what's most important, you have the calling. Journalism is the fire in your belly."

At the moment EmmaGrace thinks the fire in her belly is something she'd had for dinner... the onion in that pierogi, maybe. She is flattered by Harry's compliments, and she thanks him, but she wonders if he is any longer a competent judge. She wonders if Harry Samuels, once a competent, experienced, professional newspaperman, is all there.

Chapter 26

Even though the state line between Ohio and Pennsylvania presented no actual physical barrier—the Pennsylvania Turnpike segues into the Ohio Turnpike with little more than a shrug—as soon as Ed Plunkett drove across the line from one State to the other, he was immediately aware that he had done so. Pennsylvania literally rolls gently to its border, but when Ohio takes it up from there, it does so running flat out.

Joking to himself, Plunkett wondered if he had committed some kind of felony by carrying his zany ideas and gut-wrenching fears across a state line.

Youngstown, Ohio is north and west of Sutersberg, a two-hour trip if driving leisurely, or as Plunkett was doing, driving apprehensively, feeling as if he were dragging his feet on the pavement. Unsure of his mission.

Once he had reached Youngstown, Plunkett had no trouble locating the multi-level parking garage and the multi-storied edifice that housed the executive headquarters of *VitaBank Corp.* An elevator swept him from the garage to a marble-pillared lobby, another elevator swept him up to the twelfth floor. Plunkett found himself in the capable hands (oh how he wished) of a stunning-looking, thirty-something of an auburn-haired receptionist, who to Plunkett's sorrow handed him off to a more mature, less stunning executive aide. Probably hired by the boss's wife, Plunkett mused.

At the end of it all, he found himself seated in a very important corner office with huge windows from which one could sneer down at the town of Youngstown, below. He was invited to sit at a gigantic desk of dark wood, maybe teak—a very important looking desk even though it was entirely free of clutter. Across from him, poised, rigid-backed, in a swivel chair that matched the important desk sat an important-looking white man. Not a comment on the man's race, he was simply a very white man, obviously not a golfer or tennis player or he would be well tanned, as such important men usually were, in Plunkett's experience.

Maybe this man was more serious than other men Plunkett had dealt with. There was a pampered, powdered look to his pallid face. His hair, obviously dark at one time, was combed across his large head left to right; the hair was trying for white, too, but had only made it to gray. He was, according to the plaque on the very important desk, *VitaBank* Chief Financial Officer, J. Devlin Cosgrave.

Cosgrave offered Plunkett something to drink, which he politely refused.

"Well, then, Agent Pickett," Cosgrave said, his baritone voice fittingly important, "What can *VitaBank* do for the Federal Bureau of Investigation?"

"It's Plunkett, sir. Truthfully, I'm not here representing the Bureau or, well, actually I am but, well..."

Cosgrave reached across the desk and demanded another look at Plunkett's ID wallet. He said, "Plunkett, then. Why have you shown up here without an appointment, demanding to see me?"

"Oh, no, sir. I didn't demand, I politely asked to speak to you. I want to discuss the, uh, recent, shall we call it, incident? The incident at your Hempfield branch office? But I was hoping to keep it unofficial, sort of off the record, if that's okay with you."

"Incident? Is that what you call it, an incident?" Cosgrave was not a man who suffered fools, but he visibly forced patience on himself since the man's FBI ID looked genuine. He said, "Get on with it, then. What's this all about?"

What it was all about was this: The FBI office in the Federal Building in Pittsburgh had received a request from the *Jim Pattison Group* of London, England, owners and publishers of *The Guinness Book of World Records*. They asked the FBI to verify details they had received from an anonymous source of a robbery of a branch of *VitaBank* located in Hempfield Township, Pennsylvania, USA.

Nobody would have enjoyed more sticking a needle in a pompous ass more than Ed Plunkett. It was a joy watching Cosgrave's face as his blood pressure rose and he seemed to swell like a red balloon when he snarled, "An anonymous source?"

Plunkett nodded. He said, "Seems someone, purportedly from this very office, submitted a request that *VitaBank* be entered in *The Book* as the only bank in the world ever to be robbed by its drive-thru teller window."

"That's preposterous! No one from this office…"

"We suspect it was the Harlequin, himself, who submitted the request. Can't prove it, though."

Whatever Cosgrave was expecting to hear, it wasn't that. "The Harlequin was the source? The bandit himself? This is some sort of joke, isn't it? Someone with a weird sense of humor? Someone actually thinks this is funny? Our reputation…"

"That is the very point, Cosgrave, the very reason I've come to talk to you. It's a joke, the whole thing with the Harlequin is a joke, that seems to be the way everybody has been taking it. And by everybody I mean everyone involved in the investigation and every single citizen of Piazza County, Pennsylvania.

Cosgrave's blood pressure eased off a point or two and Plunkett let his tone of voice soften equally much.

He said, "To everyone involved, everyone, the Harlequin and all of his capers has been one big joke. Sure," Plunkett said, tossing his head, "Sure, some money was taken, but not much. Hardly any, in fact. Nobody's been hurt, no one has ever been threatened by the Harlequin, he just laughs and makes everyone else laugh. The bank employees laugh with him, the media laughs, too. Everybody has a good laugh as if nothing serious had occurred, just something to break up a boring day, that's all. Something to joke about at the water cooler or at the tavern after work."

Once again Cosgrave became insistent. "Either you're out of your mind or the people of Piazza County are."

"I admit, it sounds unlikely as hell, the ultimate in looney tunes, but I'm convinced it's exactly what's been going on. That teller, a nice young woman, a born-and-raised Pizza Countian, she's a prime example of what I'm talking about: she probably wasn't certain but I bet she was pretty sure the whole Harlequin thing was some kinda game. When she suddenly found herself in the middle of it, she simply played along."

"And you're here now to tell me...what?"

"I'm here to tell you, it wasn't her fault, what happened. She was only playing along with what she imagined was some sort of game or joke. You certainly didn't need to fire her. You shouldn't have. I'm asking you to give her her job back. It would be the right thing t'…"

Cosgrave was on his feet in the midst of a ruddy fit. "And that badge of yours gives you the right to meddle in the business of *VitaBank*?! I think not, sir. I think not. I want you out of my office right this minute! Out! Out!"

Chapter 27

Beside the ruckus that was business as usual every single mid-morning in the Sutersberg Police Station—lawyers and bail-bondsmen in, drunks and disorderlies out; phones jangling, coffee machines gurgling; hookers screaming at pimps, pimps swearing at hookers. Mayhem! —on this particular mid-morning several members of the Harlequin task force crowded into the station, as well, to bid farewell to Chief Ianuzzi and Sergeant Perkins before leaving town and heading to their respective homes. The Harlequin task force was unsuccessful and had been terminated as of the close of business the previous night. The Governor of the Commonwealth of Pennsylvania was not happy with the task force, the Attorney General was not happy with it, either; and since the Director of the FBI in Washington, D.C. was not happy with it, neither was Bluestone, the Agent in Charge of the FBI Office in Pittsburgh. Only the individual members of the task force themselves were happy. Not with the task force, but to be going home.

The two FBI agents, Sparks and Plunkett, entered via the front door of the building, as one would expect, and joined the crowd gathered in the reception area. At the same time—but much more noisily—from the 'Personnel Only' side door of the station, like a runaway freight train, State Trooper Jon 'Stump' Stepinski came crashing in, yelling at the top of his voice.

He yelled, "I got 'im, I got the Harlequin. God, he stinks, but I got 'im." As he burst through the door into the crowded reception area, he had former President

Richard Nixon by the nape of the neck and the seat of the pants. Actually, of course, it was a skinny little person with a rubber Nixon mask pulled over his head, dressed in clothes that looked longtime slept-in; a person badly in need of a bath.

At the moment Stepinski thought he had made the collar of his career. He had nabbed the Harlequin. So he thought.

Turned out Stepinski was wrong. His collar turned out to be Aristotle Barbonus, the homeless man Countians called 'the little professor' because of his encyclopedic knowledge on any number of subjects and his penchant to expound on any one of them at the drop of a hat; Aristotle Barbonus, the constant companion of Sergeant Wally Thorne USMC (retired), the County's decorated Desert Storm war hero. Sutersberg's homeless shelter was named in Thorne's honor, but the two homeless men preferred to spend their nights under the bandstand in St. Clair Park.

Chief Ianuzzi and Sergeant Perkins recognized Barbonus even before unmasking him, from the smell. So had many of the other locals in the crowded room, all of whom had begun breathing through their mouths so as not to lose their breakfasts. Once freed from Officer Stepinski's rough hands, the rubber mask was pulled from Barbonus's head, releasing a cloud of dust mixed with the odor of dirty hair. Out also came a cloud of expletives from Barbonus's mouth. Finally, out came the story as to what preceded his arrest:

Barbonus and his renowned buddy, Wally Thorne, had spent the chilly September night bundled up snug as a bug in their usual hideaway under the bandstand in St. Clair Park. Having awakened to a fresh, dewy dawn, the two homeless men set off in the direction of their usual breakfast of coffee and stale pastries at the loading dock of *Lucky Jack's Supermarket* at the foot of

Main Street hill. Their route out of the park led them past the trash barrel stationed at the park entrance, and of course they never passed a trash barrel without checking out its contents. Much to their surprise, someone had discarded several rubber masks, pieces of Halloween costumes, half-empty jars of stage makeup, and the pants to a Santa suit. Barbonus couldn't resist trying on the Richard Nixon mask and was in the midst of doing so when Officer Stepinski cruised onto the scene.

"I was compelled to don that damned mask," Barbonus groused, "Screwed once again by Nixon. I voted for him in '72, but I was all for throwing him in jail by '74, the damn crook!"

The two FBI agents stood at the back of the reception area, a little apart from the noisy crowd. Jack Sparks leaned in to speak into Ed Plunkett's ear. He said, "Looks like your message was delivered after all."

"Looks that way," Plunkett said, grinning at what to him was good news. "All of the Harlequin's disguises can probably be found in that trash barrel. None of it of any value as evidence."

"I'll bet it's all there, except for whatever those homeless guys may have removed, and like you said, no longer to be considered evidence. The Harlequin probably had it all in the trunk of his car. Which we couldn't get a warrant to search."

"Now, Jack, you know damn well, we didn't have enough evidence for a warrant. Not then and not now. The stuff in that trash barrel is just…"

"Trash. Yeah, I know, and that pleases you?"

"I've been in law enforcement most of my life, so no, I'm not pleased about that. What I am pleased about, maybe things are turning around for me. Maybe doing what I thought was the right thing actually was the right thing, for a change." He was nowhere over his failure in Youngstown.

"You haven't changed your mind about putting in for retirement, have you?"

The way that was said, even with the corners of his partner's mouth turned down and the words full of regret and displeasure, Ed Plunkett knew what his partner was thinking:

He's afraid that he would have to officially, on paper, report my conduct to the Higher Ups. Write a full report of what I did and how it might have helped scuttle the task force and send it on to the Hoover Building.

Plunkett said, "No, no. Soon as I get back to the Pittsburgh office, I'll start the retirement process rolling. Requires a mountain of paperwork, I imagine."

Sparks looked relieved. "We'll head home right after lunch, this afternoon." He expected they would be riding back to Pittsburgh together, the way they had come months ago.

"Huh uh," Ed replied. "This afternoon I have an appointment with a realtor lady who's gonna show me what's available in the way of apartments around here. Maybe even a little house. There's a bus to the 'burgh that leaves around five, and a train if I miss the bus. I'll catch one of those."

"You're thinking of moving here, to Sutersberg?"

That was his intention. "Either here in town or somewhere right nearby in the Township. I like it here in Pizza County, Jack. What's more, I feel as if Pizza County likes me. Crazy, huh? Doesn't that sound crazy? But I feel as if Pizza County likes me. I feel as if I belong here.

The End.

About the Author

Stephen was born, raised and educated in Pittsburgh, PA. After graduating from the University of Pittsburgh Dental School and serving a stint in the Army Reserve in the mid-60's, Stephen lived in, helped raise two children in and practiced family dentistry in Westmoreland County, which he jokingly calls Pizza County.

After nearly forty years there, Stephen and his wife, Shirley, finding themselves empty nesters, returned to the city of their first love, Pittsburgh, where they now reside.

www.ingramcontent.com/pod-product-compliance
Lightning Source LLC
Chambersburg PA
CBHW051346020726
47501CB00007B/2298

* 9 7 9 8 9 8 7 9 5 7 6 8 4 *